THE
REAL
SINGING
COWBOYS

CHARLIE SEEMANN

TWODOT®

Guilford, Connecticut
Helena, Montana

A · TWODOT® · BOOK

An imprint and registered trademark of Rowman & Littlefield

Distributed by NATIONAL BOOK NETWORK

Copyright © 2016 by Charles H. Seemann, Jr.

British Library Cataloguing-in-Publication Information Available

Library of Congress Cataloging-in-Publication Data available

ISBN 978-1-4930-2231-1 (paperback)
ISBN 978-1-4930-2232-8 (e-book)

♾™ The paper used in this publication meets the minimum requirements of American National Standard for Information Sciences—Permanence of Paper for Printed Library Materials, ANSI/NISO Z39.48-1992.

CONTENTS

PREFACE

There are many great western musicians active today, some of whom might be called "singing cowboys" because they perform cowboy or western music, and then there are cowboys who sing. I once asked the late Glenn Ohrlin what he thought made a good cowboy singer. He answered, "First, you gotta see how good they can ride." That is the premise on which I have based this book. My intention is not to make value judgments, but simply to look at a segment of the cowboy and western music scene that has an occupational grounding. That is, music made and performed by men and women who are, or have been, working cowboys, ranchers, packers, and horse trainers, or who have deep roots in cowboy and ranching culture that have shaped and informed their music. There has been a proliferation of western music performers since the renaissance of interest in cowboy music, poetry, crafts, and culture in the mid-1980s by events like the National Cowboy Poetry Gathering, in Elko, Nevada. The people included here are, for the most part, folks who I have had the good fortune to get to know and work with over the past forty years, and a good deal of the information in these profiles comes from interviews I conducted with them. This list is by no means complete or exhaustive; there is no way it could be. I know there are, undoubtedly, many more people out there who could and ought to be included, and to those individuals, I apologize. Omission reflects only the limits of space, time, and my personal knowledge.

ACKNOWLEDGMENTS

There are a number of people whose assistance, generosity, and encouragement I wish to acknowledge. First, of course, are all the singers who have continued and built upon western musical traditions. While many artists and family members provided photos, thanks are due to the many photographers who generously who contributed their original work: Steve Atkinson, Natalie Brown Baca, Patricia Brewer, Becki Burson, S. J. Dahlstrom, Diane Dalton, Sheri Davis, Zane Davis, Jennifer Denison and *Western Horseman* magazine, Charlie Ekburg, Marie Geibel, Guy Gillette, Lynn Martin Graton, Steve Green, Lee Gunderson, Coleen Gustafson, Ross Hecox and *Western Horseman* magazine, Bruce Hucko, Bob Kisken, Mark LaRowe, Jessica Brandi Lifland, Jens Lund, Kevin Martini-Fuller, Mindy Miller, Mary Mumma, Tony Parker, Roberta Parson, Rick Philip, Tom Pich, John Michael Reedy, Kent Reeves, Bill Rey, Chris Simon, Larry Walker, Patty Wands, Bill Watts, Sanne Lykkegarrd Wiesneck, and Ann L.Wilson. Several organizations also shared photos: Stacey Cramer-Moore and the Campfires, Cattle & Cowboys Gathering, Jody Lake and the Dee Events Center, and *Western Horseman* magazine. A huge shout-out to archivist Steve Green of the Western Folklife Center for his assistance in locating and selecting photos from the center's extensive collections. I want to thank artist Wily Matthews for the use of his painting for the cover.

I want to thank my longtime friend and colleague Patricia Hall for encouraging me to proceed with this project and poet Paul Zarzyski for being a great sounding board and providing sage advice. Thanks, too, to my literary agent Rita Rosenkranz and the great folks at Rowman & Littlefield: Erin Turner and Courtney Oppel. Finally, thanks to Katherine Hearon for her invaluable proofreading of the text. Any errors or admissions are strictly my own.

INTRODUCTION

The cowboy is the quintessential American hero, representing the values we Americans purport to hold dear: independence, honesty, hardiness, and self-reliance. The once lowly common laborer on horseback from the trail drive days of the 1800s has been transformed into a mythical icon. He has loomed large in our popular culture, literature, motion pictures, and music. But the "cowboys" of the silver screen and the Nashville recording studio have little in common with the men and women of the rural West who still make their living with horses and cattle on the land. There are, among these ranching folks, authentic cowboys and cowgirls still continuing cowboy song and musical traditions, not only performing the great old cowboy classics, but writing fresh, literate, new songs reflecting their lives on the land today. These are the people you will meet in this book.

Cowboy songs originated as the occupational folk songs of working cowboys, in the same way that songs of sailors, loggers, and miners developed in those occupations. People working in isolation and perilous conditions, left to their own creativity to entertain themselves, have always created songs and poems. Those songs reflected the often-harsh realities of the life and work of the cowboys, from the dangerous work with horses and cattle to the living conditions on the trail and in the cow camps. The cowboys also sang nonoccupational songs that dealt with other aspects of the western experience, such as immigration, outlaws, and Indians, along with popular songs of the day.

Many traditional cowboy songs were reworkings of folk and popular songs from the British Isles. For example, "The Streets of Laredo" was a cowboy version of a British and Irish broadside ballad, "The Unfortunate Rake." Likewise, "Bury Me Not on the Lone Prairie" came from an old sailor's song, "The Ocean Burial." Working cowboys also made up new songs out on the range, often setting the words to familiar traditional or popular melodies. The borrowing of older tunes and the reworking of lyrics to fit a new environment is a time-honored way of creating new songs. These ranged from anonymous folk songs like "The Old Chisholm Trail," with verses added by many different people over time, to classic compositions such as "When the Work's All Done This Fall," written by Montana cowboy poet D. J. O'Malley in 1893, and originally set to the melody of Charles K. Harris's popular Tin Pan Alley song of 1892, "After the Ball."

By the end of the 1800s, the days of the long trail drives that gave rise to cowboy songs were mostly over. With the advent of the railroads after the Civil War and the invention of barbed wire in 1874, the open range began to give way to "perimeter" ranches fenced with "the Devil's hatband." Cattle and cowboys no longer moved as freely across the open landscape of the West, and the cowboy's work changed accordingly. Rather than spending weeks and months on trail drives, he now lived part of the time in bunkhouses or cow camps and fixed fences as he tended the cattle. In this environment a rich new body of cowboy poetry and music was created. It was difficult for cowboys to carry instruments on trail drives, and most singing was unaccompanied, although smaller instruments like harmonicas and Jew's harps were common, and a fiddle could be carried in a bedroll. Bunkhouse culture provided a time and place for the guitar, mandolin, and banjo, and some of the best and well-known traditional cowboy songs come from this ranch period, such as California cowboy Curley Fletcher's "The Strawberry Roan" and Arizonian Gail I. Gardner's "The Moonshine Steer."

Cowboy songs owe much of their popularity and durability to the collectors and folklorists who preserved and published them. The first such printed collection was *Songs of the Cowboys*, a small booklet comprising twenty-three songs, privately published in 1908 by New Mexico cowboy N. Howard "Jack" Thorp. A working cowboy, Thorp developed a keen interest in the songs he heard, and in 1889 and 1890 he made a 1,500-mile journey on horseback through the cattle country of New Mexico and Texas collecting these songs, the first ballad-hunting foray into cowboy country. In 1921 he published an expanded collection of 101 songs. In 1910, two years after Thorp's booklet, folklorist John A. Lomax published *Cowboy Songs and Other Frontier Ballads*, with a foreword by Theodore Roosevelt. It was destined to become the most widely known and most influential of all cowboy song collections. These and later cowboy song anthologies took verses from oral tradition to print and made the words to songs widely available, not only to cowboys but also to other singers and musicians who added them to their own repertoires.

In the 1920s three new technologies would further transform and disseminate cowboy songs and music. These were, not coincidentally, the same technologies that expanded hillbilly music and the blues: the radio, the phonograph, and the motion picture. A number of real cowboys brought their music from the bunkhouse to the radio, and radio cowboy singers proliferated across the country. Harry "Haywire Mac" McClintock was singing cowboy and hobo songs on radio KFR and KNXC in San Francisco in 1925. Jules Verne Allen, a Texas cowboy, performed on stations WFAA in Dallas and KFI in Los Angeles. About the same time, the Arizona Wranglers were broadcasting on KTAR in Phoenix. John I. White, who was not a real cowboy, was one of the first to adopt the persona and repertoire, and he was featured on New York stations WEAF and WOR as the "Lonesome Cowboy," starting in 1926.

Record companies, sensing a specialty market as they had with hillbilly music, quickly began recording cowboy songs. Concert singer Bentley Ball, by no stretch a cowboy, was the first to record cowboy songs, namely "The Dying Cowboy" and "Jesse James" in 1919. Citybilly singers Charles Nabell and Vernon Dalhart both tried recording cowboy songs in 1924, but it was a ranch-reared Texan, Carl T. Sprague, who brought both authenticity and success with his 1925 recording of "When the Work's All Done This Fall." The recording was very popular, selling perhaps as many as nine hundred thousand copies.

Some authentic cowboys followed Sprague into the recording studio, including the Cartwright Brothers and Jules Verne Allen, and Oklahoma rancher Otto Gray. A herd of drugstore cowboys jumped on the chuck wagon, and through their affectation of cowboy attire and the popularization of western music they further enhanced the progressively romanticized image of the cowboy.

The third new medium, the motion picture, was also quick to join the stampede, but the singing cowboy had to wait for the advent of the talkie. The first movie singing cowboy was Ken Maynard, an expert horseman and stunt rider who had once performed with Pawnee Bill's Wild West Show before coming to Hollywood to become a silent movie cowboy actor. In October 1929 he was featured in the B western *The Wagon Master*, in which he played guitar and sang "The Lonestar Trail." He was soon eclipsed by more accomplished singers such as Gene Autry, Tex Ritter, and the King of the Cowboys, Roy Rogers.

As the cowboy image was appropriated by the larger popular culture, cowboy music underwent significant changes. While cowboy songs had traditionally been sung unaccompanied or with simple guitar accompaniment, audiences had become accustomed to more sophisticated musical arrangements from professional performers. Cowboy singers were competing in new media arenas with other contemporary musical forms, ranging from jazz and big-band swing to blues and hillbilly. As cowboy music moved from the trail and cow camp to radio, records, and movies, influences from other forms of popular music found their way into the genre. By the 1930s cowboy singers regularly performed with bands that included guitars, fiddles, accordions, basses, and even horns on occasion, and musicians incorporated elements of pop music in their playing. During the golden era of the celluloid singing cowboys, from the 1930s to the 1950s, Hollywood attracted scores of actors, stuntmen, musicians, and songwriters, and a thriving western music scene developed in Southern California. There were quite a few active "cowboy" or "western" groups, but the best-known and most influential group to emerge was the Sons of the Pioneers, cofounded by Roy Rogers. The Pioneers combined close-harmony trio and quartet singing with sophisticated guitar and fiddle influenced by the playing of jazz guitarist Django Reinhardt and violinist Stephane Grappelli.

Two of the group's members, Bob Nolan and Tim Spencer, were among commercial western music's most talented songwriters, composing such numbers as "Cool Water" and "Tumblin' Tumbleweeds" for the group, creating music more appropriately called "western" than "cowboy." Along with Tin Pan Alley songwriters such as Billy Hill, Fred Rose, and Nat Vincent and Fred Howard (the "Happy Chappies"), they created a new a new genre of songs that, unlike the more realistic traditional cowboy songs, painted a highly romanticized portrait of an idyllic West. The Sons of the Pioneers appeared in several movies singing behind Roy Rogers and others. The strong influence of the Sons of the Pioneers can be heard today in the singing and playing of groups like Riders in the Sky and the Sons of the San Joaquin.

Although working cowboys prior to the twentieth century were almost always male, women became involved in commercial western music early on. The first cowgirl to record was Billie Maxwell, from Arizona ranching country, who recorded six solo sides for the Victor label in 1929, including "A Cowboy's Wife" and "The Arizona Girl I Left Behind Me." There were other female singers, such as Kitty Lee, who performed with her husband, Powder River Jack Lee, and Buerl Sisney, "the Lonesome Cowgirl." The first real cowgirl singing "star" was Arkansas native Patsy Montana. Born Ruby Blevins, she began her career in Los Angeles, performing with a trio called the Montana Cowgirls. She later joined up with the Kentucky Ramblers, who changed their name to the Prairie Ramblers to enhance a western image. In 1935 she recorded "I Want to Be a Cowboy's Sweetheart," which became the first big hit for a female country singer. Her success opened the way for other cowgirl singers who followed her, including Jenny Lou Carson, Texas Ruby, and the Girls of the Golden West. Patsy's influence can still be heard today in the singing of contemporary artists such as Suzy Bogguss, Liz Masterson, and Eli Barsi.

After the last singing cowboy films were made in the 1950s, popular interest in things cowboy ebbed, including cowboy and western music. Some western artists moved into mainstream country music, and even though the term "country and western" was still used, not much western influence remained in commercial country music. The rise of rock 'n' roll also captured the country's attention. A few groups, such as the Wagonmasters, the Flying W Wranglers, and the perennially reconstituted Sons of the Pioneers, continued to perform, but mostly at dude ranches and western theme parks. A few traditional performers found a place in the folk music revival of the late 1950s and early 1960s. Among these were Glenn Ohrlin, a former buckaroo, rodeo rider, and rancher based in Arkansas, and Harry Jackson, who recorded an album of cowboy songs for Folkways Records.

The 1970s saw the first signs of a cowboy and western resurgence. Willie Nelson released his western-themed *Red Headed Stranger* album in 1975 and was soon joined by Waylon Jennings, Tompall Glaser, and others in the so-called outlaw movement. In 1977 the western singing group Riders in the Sky was formed in Nashville, performing in the style of the Sons of the Pioneers, adding a comic twist to their stage shows. They have proven to be one of western music's most enduring ensembles. It was also during the 1970s that champion rodeo bronc rider Chris LeDoux began gaining a following with his rodeo-themed songs on his own Lucky Man Label, and he became really well-known when Garth Brooks mentioned him in his 1989 song "Much Too Young (to Feel This Damn Old)."

The 1980s also saw a revival of interest in the oral tradition of cowboy poetry; that had a parallel development with traditional cowboy songs, which were really just poems set to music. In 1985 a group of folklorists, led by Jim Griffith from Arizona and Hal Cannon from Utah, organized the first Cowboy Poetry Gathering, held in Elko, Nevada. Although the emphasis was on recited poetry of working cowboys, there was a strong musical and song component. State folklorists in the West did extensive fieldwork to locate and identify traditional cowboy poets, singers, and musicians, and they were invited to Elko. The gathering was intended to be a one-time event, but the response from the ranching community, the general public, and the media was so overwhelming that it became an annual event. In 2000 the United States Senate proclaimed the Elko event the National Cowboy Poetry Gathering, largely in response to the fact that it had spawned several hundred similar cowboy poetry and music events throughout the West. Some have called this a "cowboy renaissance."

In 2015 the Elko gathering celebrated its thirty-first anniversary. In addition to reacquainting old-timers with traditional poetry and music, the event has inspired younger generations to write and perform material drawn from their contemporary western and ranching experience. The rekindled interest in western writing and music inspired by the National Cowboy Poetry Gathering and its progeny has bolstered the careers of some of the older, traditional cowboy singers. The late Glenn Ohrlin, the late Buck Ramsey, and Duane Dickinson have earned a special place in the hearts of cowboy music audiences. Ohrlin and Ramsey both received National Heritage Fellowships from the National Endowment for the Arts, the nation's highest award given to traditional and folk artists. Canadian rancher and singer Ian Tyson has become something of a western icon for his literate and powerful songs about life in the West. Similarly, Don Edwards, Michael Martin Murphey, and Red Steagall have all developed loyal followings.

As the cowboy and western music revival picked up steam, a supporting infrastructure began to emerge. The proliferation of cowboy music and poetry events created a circuit that provided artists with venues and performing opportunities throughout the year. In 1988 the Western Music Association, patterned loosely after the Country Music Association and the International Bluegrass Music Association, was formed. Specialty record labels, like Colorado-based Western Jubilee Records, featured the work of cowboy and western artists, including Don Edwards, the Sons of the San Joaquin, and Rich O'Brien. Many other artists have created their own small, independent record labels, and the level of activity continues to increase.

It is surprising that what might be thought an anachronistic form of folk song not only persists into the twenty-first century but continues to inspire new music in the tradition. In the 1960s no one could have predicted that cowboy and western music would see the resurgence it has enjoyed during the past three decades, taking its place as a cherished regional subgenre on the American musical scene, along with Cajun music, blues, and bluegrass. But after more than thirty years of popular revival, there is no sign that the movement is losing steam. In fact, it continues to grow, with new events, festivals, and performers appearing all the time. Most importantly, the music not only continues to reflect the past but also provides a medium for the men and women who still make a living on the land today, such as those included in this volume, to tell their own stories of their contemporary experience in the changing West.

JESSE BALLANTYNE

Jesse Ballantyne was born in Saskatchewan, Canada, on a ranch homesteaded by his grandfather in 1905. His family raised cattle, horses, and grain. He started riding at age five and grew up running cattle with his father and brother. He took his first paying cowboy job in the summer of his fourteenth year. In his twenties he rodeoed as a saddle bronc rider while continuing to work on the ranch. He has cowboyed for outfits in Montana, Wyoming, and California. In Montana he also served as a deputy state brand inspector.[1] Now living in Sheridan, Wyoming, he spends his time starting colts, training horses, and day working in addition to playing music.

Jesse got his first guitar when he was fifteen, and he learned to play. Eventually he started writing songs, and writing songs and performing have become as important a part of his life as horses and cattle. His finely crafted songs portray cowboy life through the eyes of a working cowboy, recognizable by cowboys but accessible to all listeners.

Jesse has performed at events such as the National Cowboy Poetry Gathering in Elko, Nevada, and the Texas Cowboy Poetry Gathering in Alpine, and at sites such as the National Cowboy and Western Heritage Museum in Oklahoma City, Oklahoma. In 2003 he released his first album, *Cowboy Serenade*, to great acclaim. Jesse says, "I want to continue with the horses, I want to continue with the music . . . Probably won't be starting colts when I'm seventy, but I definitely want to be involved with horses . . . it's the horses, the cowboying, and the music."[2]

MIKE BECK

Mike Beck grew up in Monterey County, California, old Californio ranching country. He got his first horse when he was nine, a chestnut mare named Candy, and he was hooked. His love of music followed close behind, when at thirteen he attended the Monterey Pop Festival and decided he had to learn to play the guitar. Ever since, his life has combined horses and music, his songs reflecting his life as a musician and working cowboy and horse trainer.

By the time he was eighteen Mike had hooked up with local horseman Roy Forzoni and was working with horses at the Hidden Hills Stables in Carmel Valley. It was through Forzoni that he would be introduced to the legendary horsemen Bill and Tom Dorrance, from whom he learned about training horses. Mike recalls, "I lived with Bill Dorrance at his ranch, and he became a major influence on my life . . . he helped me with horses, cattle, and roping and I would say Bill was the best teacher I ever had." He also met another California horseman, Bryan Neubert, "who helped me so much, and I would go to his parents' house and ride colts with him there too." Neubert got him a job in Nevada on the legendary two-million-acre Spanish Ranch working for Bill Kane. Mike would ride out with the wagon sometimes for weeks at a time. He says, "It was my Yale and Harvard." He worked on ranches in Nevada, California, and Montana. Mike began using the skills he had learned from the Dorrances and Neubert to offer his own horse clinics, eventually in sixteen states and six foreign countries.[1]

Meanwhile, Mike continued to pursue his music career, applying the same principles he learned from training horses to shape his playing and songwriting. In an article in *Western Horseman*, he said, "Bill taught me that to do something well, you have to live it, breathe it, never stop

thinking about it, and then start over the next day. If I'm learning a new melody, I remind myself to go slow, take my time and put it all together. That's the same thing Bill taught me to do with horses."[2] Growing up in California, Mike was influenced musically by the Byrds, Buffalo Spring-field, and Buck Owens. He is a consummate guitar player and stylist and is often asked to conduct guitar workshops at festivals. Ramblin' Jack Elliott has said, "Mike Beck plays guitar like a Byrd. His strings do things that mine could never do. They obey the slightest finger-touch commands like a fine reining horse."[3] Mike is also recognized as one of the best contemporary writers of western and Americana songs. *Western Horseman* magazine included two of Mike's songs, "In Old California" and "Don't Tell Me," in its list of the thirteen best cowboy songs of all time.

Mike working a horse on the ground

Mike on horseback in Montana

Mike released his first album, *Mariposa Wind*, in 2001 to wide acclaim. Since then he has released six more albums. His latest, *Tribute*, celebrates veterans and rescued horses; proceeds from sales of the CD support the Joyful Horse Project's Veteran's Program in Austin, Texas, which brings former combat soldiers together with horses that are being rehabilitated for adoption.

In addition to his solo career, Mike has also led the Bohemian Saints, a popular old-fashioned guitar band. They perform mostly original material composed by Mike, reflecting the influences of the Byrds, the Flying Burrito Brothers, and the Rolling Stones.

ADRIAN BRANNAN

Adrian Brannan was just fourteen years old and had been playing guitar for only two weeks when she first stepped on stage to perform. She was at the Monterey, California, Cowboy Poetry and Music Festival with her sister, Liz, who was selling some of her braided rawhide horse gear. Adrian decided to give the open mic stage a try, and she was soon a young singing sensation on the festival scene. About that same time she began writing songs, and many of them reflected her western upbringing. Her father was a working cowboy and saddlemaker, and she was around horses her entire life. When she was around two and a half, her father took a job buckarooing on a northern Nevada ranch near Elko. Her family eventually moved to northern California to run a cow-calf operation there. Adrian grew up spending many of her days horseback, working cattle and horses with her father and her sister. She was starting yearlings, doctoring cows, and roping, but that wasn't enough. She wanted to try her hand at rodeo bronc riding, which she did until she suffered some serious injuries.

Along the way she began to perform using just her first name, Adrian, and then added "Buckaroogirl," as she is now known. *Western Horseman* magazine chose "The Will James Days," from her first CD, *Highway 80*, as one of the thirteen best cowboy songs of all time. Adrian's second CD, *Boots and Pearls*, was produced by singer-song-writer Tom Russell, who said in *Cowboy Way* magazine, "I heard the clear potential. I was impressed that she has such a great voice and was so at ease on stage. . . . Adrian is the breath of strong fresh air that the cowboy music scene needs. I was honored to have worked with her." Adrian's third CD, *Buckaroogirl*, was released in 2012. *Ranch and Reata* magazine called the CD "a gift to all of us who enjoy real western music. She is, in fact, the real deal." Adrian says her songs reflect her experiences and those of the cowboys she works with and lives around.[1]

DALE BURSON AND FAMILY

DISCOGRAPHY

Burson Family Ranch, 2001
Dancing with Daddy, 2004
The Heart, 2015

AWARDS

National Cowboy and
    Western Heritage Museum,
    Wrangler Award for
    Outstanding Original
    Western Composition, "A
    Life More Than This," 2004

Dale Burson, a fourth-generation rancher, makes his home on his Hartley County ranch in the Texas Panhandle near the town of Channing, where he runs both cow-calf and yearling operations. Influenced by his musical grandmother, he started playing music in his teens. Dale says, "In summer, Dad would send each of us kids to a camp on the ranch to work. With no radio or TV, you needed something to do at night."[1] Dale taught himself to play guitar, fiddle, mandolin, and banjo. In 2000 he came to the National Cowboy Poetry Gathering, in Elko, Nevada, at the request of the widow of Buck Ramsey, who asked him to recite one of Buck's poems in the "Follow the Cow Trail" stage presentation honoring Buck, who had passed away in 1998. His performance attracted the attention of musician and singer Red Steagall, who later asked Dale to come to Fort Worth, Texas, to play guitar and sing harmony with him at his annual Cowboy Gathering and Western Swing Festival. This was the start of a musical partnership that has had Dale touring North America with Steagall for more than two decades.

The Bursons have continued the family's musical tradition as his daughter, Brittany, and son, Ross, have joined Dale to perform around the country as the popular Burson Family. Ross plays guitar and mandolin, and Brittany plays fiddle and mandolin.

Dale released his first album, *Burson Family Ranch*, in 2001. In 2004 he received a Wrangler Award from the National Cowboy and Western Heritage Museum for Outstanding Original Western Composition for his song "A Life More Than This," which was included on his second album, *Dancing with Daddy*. In 2015 he released *The Heart*.

Left: Dale Burson and Red Steagall play around the campfire.
Right: Dale with his horse in Monument Valley

LYLE CUNNINGHAM

Lyle "Wild Horse" Cunningham was a legendary, larger-than-life character in Montana. He was born on July 21, 1928, in Miles City, the son of Thomas and Rose Cunningham, well-known livestock producers in southeastern Montana near the small communities of Ismay and Locate. As he grew up, Lyle worked on various ranches, rode in rodeos, produced rodeos, and owned bars. He enlisted in the United States Army during World War II, and after the war he returned to Miles City and the surrounding area to fulfill his lifelong dream of being a cowboy.[1] He got the name "Wild Horse" from his days as a mustanger, rounding up wild horses off the range and selling them. He had a colorful life and a checkered career. He owned and operated the old O. K. Corral livery stable in Miles City. It was during this time he produced rodeos near the old Leon Park Night Club. He and his first wife were married on horseback in the rodeo arena. Lyle was best known for owning one of Montana's most notorious bars, the Wild Horse Pavilion, which was also, as he delighted in calling it, "a whorehouse," until it was closed down.

Lyle was gifted in reciting cowboy poetry as well as playing guitar and singing the old cowboy songs. Later on in years, he entertained at cowboy poetry gatherings all over the West, including Cowboy Songs and Range Ballads, in Cody, Wyoming, and the National Cowboy Poetry Gathering in Elko, Nevada.[2]

JAY DALTON

Nevada cowboy, rancher, auctioneer, and singer Jay Dalton was born and reared on the ranch his family established in 1895 in Clover Valley at the foot of the East Humboldt Mountains in Elko County, Nevada. He represents the fifth generation on the ranch. Jay started cowboying early, dragging meadows on the ranch when he was about eight years old, and has been at it ever since. As a boy he always wanted to play the guitar, so for his eighth birthday his mother bought him one and insisted he take lessons to learn to play it, which he did for about eight years. The first time he recalls playing for people outside the family was when he was in the second grade, when he played for his fellow students. The first time he played in a bar he was twelve. He was with his parents in a bar in Montana, where someone was playing, and his mother asked if Jay could borrow the guitar and play something. In 1994 cowboy poet Baxter Black invited him to open for him at the National Cowboy Poetry Gathering in Elko, Nevada, where Jay has appeared often since. He learned a lot of cowboy songs from his family, particularly some handed down from his great-grandfather, as well as from old records his great-grandmother had. When he was a sophomore in high school, he entered a Future Farmers of America talent contest and got more interested in performing.

Jay was certified as an auctioneer when he was eighteen. He became interested in the auction business, attending many bull sales, farm sales, and county fairs with his family. He picked up his "chant" from these events and perfected it in high school and was asked to assist in calling bids at the 1998 Elko County Fair. Following the sale,

the folks involved with the 4-H program at the time decided to raise a scholarship for their budding young auctioneer. In 1999 Jay graduated from the Western College of Auctioneering in Billings, Montana, and was named the outstanding student in his class. When he returned to the ranch, he started Dalton Auction Service. He later studied at the University of Nevada in Reno, where he earned a bachelor of science degree in agricultural and applied economics in 2003. He regularly plays for family functions, for community parties, and around the campfire, and occasionally for trail rides. In addition to his other skills, Jay is a pilot and uses a plane for work on the ranch where he lives with his wife, Rebecca.

Branding at the ranch

KEVIN DAVIS

DISCOGRAPHY

This Cowboy's Heart, 2001
Every Horse I Ever Rode, 2008
This Cowboy Life, 2015

AWARDS

Academy of Western Artists,
   Will Rogers Rising Star
   Award, 2001

Singer-songwriter Kevin Davis hails from Walters, Oklahoma. He comes from a family of horsemen and got his first pay for cowboying when he was twelve. He has been a champion rodeo cowboy for many years, competing in bareback and saddle bronc riding, calf roping, and team roping from the age of eighteen. He has been a working cowboy for more than twenty years, doing day work mostly, all over Oklahoma and Texas. Kevin grew up around music in his family and remembers his grandfather's stories of traveling horseback to play fiddle for dances. He developed a love of music standing in the seat of his father's pickup and listening to lots of country music on the radio.

After he got hurt rodeoing and was laid up for a while, Kevin decided to use the time to learn to play guitar. He began writing songs at the same time he mastered the guitar, drawing from his experiences and people he has known. The first time he remembers actually playing for other people was while he was doing day work for Leroy Anderson at the Hereford Ranch. He had gone out with the wagon, taking his guitar with him, and was talked into singing some songs at the campfire. The guys liked what they heard and encouraged him, and it changed his life. With his first album, Kevin won the Will Rogers Rising Star Award from the Academy of Western Artists. He has become a favorite at cowboy poetry and music events such as the Texas Cowboy Poetry Gathering and the Durango Cowboy Poetry Gathering.

STEPHANIE DAVIS

DISCOGRAPHY

Stephanie Davis, 1993
I'm Pullin' Through, 1996
River of No Return, 1998
Crocus in the Snow, 2004
Home for the Holidays, 2005
Western Bling, 2009
Western Bliss, 2009

Stephanie Davis is a fourth-generation Montanan. Her father's immigrant parents homesteaded a little ranch near Fishtail. Stephanie says,

> With nine kids, brutal winters, and often desperately hard times, they somehow managed to eke out a living with remarkable humor and grace. My dad and uncle spent their summers barefoot, high in the Beartooth Mountains, looking after some 5,000 sheep for the local grazing association. This was well before the luxuries of flashlights, sleeping bags, etc. "A rifle and a bag of beans," as my dad used to say. The spellbinding stories they would tell around the campfires of my own youth were, I believe, a huge influence on my wish to write about the "real" West, vs. the Hollywood version.[1]

Stephanie is known for writing some of the best, most evocative and literate contemporary western songs. Western artist Don Edwards once said, "Up until a few years ago I was one of those who thought that all the great western songs had been written, but that was before I met Stephanie Davis."[2] Stephanie moved to Nashville, Tennessee, hoping to get a start in the music industry. She soon established herself as a performer and released an album for Asylum Records in 1993 that included the single "It's All in the Heart," which reached number seventy-two on the country charts. However, it was as a songwriter that she had her greatest success, penning songs that were recorded by Shelby Lynne, Waylon Jennings, Martina McBride, and many others. Most notably, Garth Brooks recorded three of her songs: "Wolves," "The Gift," and "We Shall Be Free." He also hired her as his opening act and even made her part of his band for a time.[3]

Stephanie is also an accomplished fiddler.

Stephanie with her cow dogs at her Montana ranch

Eventually Stephanie, like many other artists, became disillusioned with the Nashville recording scene. In the mid-1990s she returned to her roots in her native Montana, where she bought a small ranch and set up a writing studio in a one-room cabin.

She began writing more personal material and started her own label, Recluse Records. In addition to becoming a favorite featured performer at cowboy poetry and music events, Stephanie has frequently appeared as a guest on Garrison Keillor's *A Prairie Home Companion*. In 2015 she relocated once again, this time to Austin, Texas, to further pursue her writing and performing career.

GENO DELAFOSE

Southwest Louisiana has a long ranching history that goes back to the eighteenth century. Folklorist Nick Spitzer has described the local culture as an amalgam of French, Spanish, English, and colonials who settled the Gulf region from Florida to Texas as farmers and ranchers. Horses and cattle have always been an important part of this culture, and early on there were cattle drives along the Gulf Coast to New Orleans. Geno Delafose comes from the community of French-speaking Creoles of color who created zydeco music, a blend of blues, rhythm and blues, and Cajun music indigenous to the Louisiana Creoles and the native people of Louisiana.

Geno was born and reared in the small town of Eunice. Son of the late legendary zydeco master John Delafose, Geno combines being a touring musician with running his Double D Ranch outside of Eunice, where he raises cattle and quarter horses. Geno started playing *frottoir* (rubboard) in his father's band, the Eunice Playboys, later picking up drums, then accordion, and singing in Creole French and English. Geno has become a worldwide star, headlining the New Orleans Jazz and Heritage Festival and touring Europe and North America. He's been featured with his band, French Rockin' Boogie, in John Sayles's acclaimed film *Passion Fish* and on the soundtrack of the film *Eve's Bayou*. In 2010 he and his band were invited to perform at the National Cowboy Poetry Gathering in Elko, Nevada.

Geno explains that he plays the single-row and triple-row diatonic button accordions for more traditional French-style tunes. He switches to the powerful big piano accordion, made famous by Clifton Chenier, for zydeco house rocking. The Delafose band is a meeting point of Cajun influences and R&B, and its stylistic range makes French Rockin' Boogie one of the most interesting groups to come out of the Louisiana musical revival. During an interview in the late 1990s, Geno said, "We have that old country feel, that soft swing, and then we have that loud, bluesy, get-down thing going on, too. We try to mix it up, give everybody something they can dance to."[1]

Geno with his band, French Rockin' Boogie

DUANE DICKINSON

Duane Dickinson grew up on a family ranch near Scobey, in northeastern Montana. He learned cowboy songs and romantic nineteenth-century ballads from his father, eventually accumulating an incredible repertoire of songs. Cowboy poet and singer Buck Ramsey used to call Duane "a walking encyclopedia of cowboy songs." Duane ranched most of his life, until selling his ranch in Ryegate, Montana, and semi-retiring. In 1982 Duane attended the annual Cowboy Songs and Range Ballads event at the Buffalo Bill Historical Center in Cody, Wyoming, where his singing and knowledge of classic cowboy songs immediately attracted people's attention and admiration. He soon became a frequent performer at cowboy poetry and music events around the West. Duane, along with a handful of older cowboy singers like Glenn Ohrlin, Walt LaRue, and Lyle Cunningham, was an authentic link to the old-time cowboys of the turn of the century from whom they learned their songs. In 2003 western performers Liz Masterson and Sean Blackburn took Duane into the Ravens Records recording studio in Englewood, Colorado, where he recorded seventeen songs for his only CD, *When the Work's All Done This Fall*. Duane retired from performing publicly and resided in Moses Lake, Washington. Duane passed away on May 18, 2016.

JUNI FISHER

Born in Strathmore in the San Joaquin Valley of California, Juni Fisher grew up in a farming family and around horses. Throughout her school years she won honors from 4-H and the Future Farmers of America. She began singing while in elementary school, in a trio with her sisters, and began playing guitar at age seven. She wrote her first song when she was eight. She graduated from the College of the Sequoias in Visalia, where she studied equine science. She rode young horses for her customers and became known as a good horse show "catch rider." In college she garnered top honors at intercollegiate and quarter horse shows. Meanwhile, she was earning horse show entry money by singing big-band standards in a dance orchestra.[1]

In her early adult years, Juni apprenticed with a cowhorse trainer and worked with a variety of cowhorses, from snaffle bitters to bridle horses. She won her first Snaffle Bit Futurity in 1981 and her first Bridle Horse Championship in 1983, while working on a cow-calf operation and running a roping arena. Her bridle horses did day work on the ranch and competed on weekends. If there was a campfire gathering with music, Juni was there with her guitar, singing western songs she had learned from her father.[2]

In 1984 she moved to Santa Ynez, California, to work for a cutting horse trainer. A local band asked her to play rhythm guitar and sing lead and backup, and soon she was working LA-area clubs with a country dance band, playing western and cowboy music.

Juni's ability to ride at speed across the hills found her working as a foxhunting professional, and she accepted a one-year position with a hunt club in Tennessee. Point-to-point racing, steeplechasing, and horse trials took the place of riding cowhorses while she honed her songwriting skills among Nashville's finest.[3]

Her first western release, *Tumbleweed Letters* (1999), reached Monterey Cowboy Poetry and Music Festival director Gary Brown in late 2003. He shared Juni's music with other promoters and soon Juni shifted to music full time as her profession. She now performs at major festivals and concert venues of all sizes across the United States, but she still spends saddle time on her cutting horse, keeping her tuned up for competition.

Juni on her horse Silk

AWARDS

Western Music Association, Crescendo Award, 2005

Academy of Western Artists, Western Music Female Vocalist of the
  Year, 2005

Western Music Association, Female Vocalist of the Year, 2006

Western Music Association, Song of the Year, "I Hope She'll Love Me," 2007

Western Music Association, Songwriter of the Year, 2008

National Cowboy and Western Heritage Museum, Wrangler Award for
  Outstanding Western Album, *Gone for Colorado*, 2008

Western Music Association, Traditional Album of the Year, *Gone for
  Colorado*, 2009

Western Music Association, Female Performer of the Year, 2009

Western Music Association, Song of the Year, "Yakima," 2011

Western Music Association, Female Performer of the Year, 2011

Western Music Association, Entertainer of the Year, 2011

True West magazine, Best Solo Performer and Editor's Choice, 2012

NRCHA Celebrity Cow Horse Challenge champion, 2012

Western Music Association, Song of the Year, "Listen," 2013

Western Writers of America, Spur Award for Best Western Song, "Still
  There," 2014

BROWNIE FORD

Thomas Edison "Brownie" Ford was born in 1904 in the Oklahoma Territory town of Gum Springs. He was half Comanche. As a child he spent most of his time with an uncle who was in the horse-trading business. When he was eight his uncle started bringing him along on cattle drives. Brownie became interested in music early as he listened to the fiddle and guitar music of his family and neighbors, and he began playing the guitar himself. He started breaking horses at about age eleven. The following year he joined Indian Joe Keith's Wild West Show, a split-off from Buffalo Bill's Wild West Show. He worked as a bronc rider for the show while it toured during the summer. For a short time he also traveled with the M. L. Clark and Sons Great Combined Wagon Show. In the off-season he cared for the animals.[1]

During World War I Brownie caught wild horses for the army. In the 1920s he worked in traveling medicine shows and circuses as a pitchman, performer, and musician.[2] When the Depression came Brownie moved on to the rodeo circuit, riding broncs and bulls, and working as a pioneer rodeo clown. The rodeos also provided a venue for him to perform as a musician. While he was working with traveling shows and competing on the rodeo circuit, he worked as a "woods cowboy" in the brushy, swampy cattle country of southeast Texas and southwest Louisiana. Brownie said, "Hell, anybody can punch cows on dry land; you might call what we do down here high-water herding."[3]

In 1972 Brownie moved to Hebert, Louisiana, where he repaired saddles, made horse tack, and produced cattle hide–bottomed chairs. Eventually, he and his wife opened a bait and food store on the shore of Bayou LaFourche.[4] He continued to perform as a musician, appearing

at festivals and taking part in Louisiana's Artists in Schools program. In 1983 he performed at the Library of Congress as part of its *American Cowboy* exhibit. In 1983 and 1984 he brought his huge repertoire of old-time cowboy songs to the Old Puncher's Reunion/Cowboy Tour, produced by the National Council for the Traditional Arts, in which eight working cowboys from Louisiana to Hawaii presented their brand of music, stories, and poetry to audiences on two tours in the West.[5] In 1987 Brownie was awarded the prestigious National Heritage Fellowship by the National Endowment for the Arts. In 1990 he released his only solo album, for Flying Fish Records, *Stories from Mountains, Swamps, and Honky-Tonks*, a mixture of field recordings, live performances, and studio recordings. Brownie passed away in 1996.

RYAN FRITZ

DISCOGRAPHY

*Cow Camps and Street
    Lamps*, 1998
When a Cowboy Calls, 2002
One Last Horse, 2005
Wind Blown Buckaroo, 2013
Keeper of the West, 2016

Ryan Fritz, singer, songwriter, working cowboy, and rancher, was born in British Columbia and reared in southern Alberta, and he began both cowboying and playing the guitar while he was in high school. Ryan's mother and sisters played piano; there was always someone playing music in the household. His father always sang along with the radio in his pickup, and Ryan says that singing passed on to him. During his summer vacation between grades eleven and twelve, he worked for a pack outfit in the Rocky Mountains near Jasper, Alberta, as a horse wrangler and packer. Ryan says, "I had my guitar with me and was talked into playing for the guests one night. It went over well, and I think I played for every group that rode in there after that."[1]

After graduating from high school at seventeen, he quickly got a job at the legendary Gang Ranch in the Chilcotin region of British Columbia, the second-largest ranch in Canada, making $800 a month. Ryan took his guitar with him from ranch to ranch while he was making the cowboy circle working the big outfits. He recalls, "I was pretty much the only means of entertainment in those camps, with no power or phones."[2] In the evenings he would sneak off with his guitar and work on writing his own songs.

In 1998 he was working for the Douglas Lake Cattle Company, Canada's largest ranch, when he thought that after six years of writing and playing his own songs, he should try recording some of them. His fellow cowboys helped scrape together the money to make the recording, and the result was *Cow Camps and Street Lamps*. They sold 300 copies in fairly short order, and the boys were paid back. Ryan would eventually record five albums.

By 2002 Ryan had a wife and three kids and decided it was time to leave the big outfits. He wanted his kids to be intimately involved with ranching, which is difficult on the big outfits. Alberta land was too expensive, so they looked to the far east side of Saskatchewan. He and his family ran custom cattle for the first few years and then started their own herd just in time for the mad cow disease outbreak. Today they run around five hundred stocker cattle, and Ryan also does custom cowboy work in the grazing months along with his sons, looking after large herds of cattle horseback. Ryan has continued to combine being a rancher and cowboy with being a musician, and says he doesn't think he could be one without the other. Today he performs at numerous cowboy events in Canada and the United States.

GILLETTE BROTHERS

DISCOGRAPHY

Home Ranch, 1992
Cinch Up Your Riggin', 1994
Lone Star Trail, 1997
The Gillette Brothers, Live From the Camp Street Cafe and Store, 2001
Ridin' with Dayton, 2003
Many Long Miles to Ride, 2006
Cowboys, Minstrels, and Medicine Shows, 2010
Leaving Cheyenne, 2012

BOOKS

A Family of the Land: The Texas Photography of Guy Gillette (the brothers' father), with text by Andy Wilkinson, 2013

The Gillette brothers, Guy and Pipp, moved from Yonkers, New York, in 1983, to Lovelady, Texas, to take over their grandfather's Texas ranch, which they had inherited. Their grandfather, V. H. "Hoyt" Porter, started the ranch in 1912. Although the brothers grew up in New York, they spent their summer vacations working with their grandfather on the ranch. Cattle ranching had been in their blood ever since. They continued to run a commercial cow-calf operation much the same as their grandfather. The ranch was run-down, and they undertook the task of refurbishing the ranch and the old homestead. They also renovated Camp Street, in Crockett, Texas, a pool hall and barbershop also built and owned by their grandfather. They turned it into a music venue called the Camp Street Cafe and Store, where they presented live music.

As teenagers they put together a band called the Roadrunners that featured a young Diane Keaton as the lead singer. Keaton eventually left the band to star in the musical *Hair* and was discovered by Woody Allen. The brothers continued to play the coffeehouse circuit up and down the East Coast and throughout the Midwest from 1968 to 1983. After relocating to Texas, they continued to entertain audiences at their Camp Street venue and across the country with their signature mixture of folk, blues, and cowboy songs. Both brothers being instrumentalists, they performed on guitars, banjos, harmonicas, kazoos, and the bones, at which Guy was a virtuoso. They released their first album, *Home Ranch*, in 1992, and eventually went on to release seven more. They became favorites on the cowboy poetry and music circuit, performing at the National Cowboy Poetry Gathering in Elko, Nevada, and similar events in Prescott, Arizona; Cody, Wyoming; and Alpine, Texas, among others.

Guy and Pipp Gillette playing music on their porch

The brothers were not only ranchers and musicians. Once ensconced at the ranch, they became cooks. In the early 1990s they traveled to a ranch rodeo where they met some great chuck wagon cooks and decided they should try their hand at it. They bought a chuck wagon and, with

Pipp Gillette

advice from culinary friends, were soon winning chuck wagon cooking competitions themselves. They found that performing music along with cooking was a good combination, and as Pipp says, "It started making financial sense." They did so well they were awarded the National Cowboy Symposium's American Cowboy Culture Chuck Wagon Award in 1998.

In 2005 they represented the state of Texas at the World Expo in Japan, and in 2008 they were invited to perform at the Smithsonian Folklife Festival in Washington, DC. Over the years, they have received numerous awards and honors. The Gillette Brothers have been profiled in feature articles in publications such as *Texas Highways*, *Texas Monthly*, and the *Houston Chronicle*. They have appeared on television in *Texas Country Reporter*, *Good Morning Texas*, and CMT's Christmas special *Christmas in Cowboy Country*, hosted by Clint Black. Their music is featured on the soundtrack to the 1995 documentary *Gathering Remnants*, by filmmaker Kendall Nelson.

Guy Porter Gillette passed away in 2013. Pipp has continued to perform solo and with other musicians at Camp Street, at cowboy poetry and music events, and at the National Storytelling Festival in Jonesborough, Tennessee.

D. W. GROETHE

DISCOGRAPHY

Notes from the Hinterland (cassette), 1995
There's a Place, 2000
Tales from West River, 2002
Whatever It Takes, 2004

BOOKS

A Charlie Creek Christmas and Other Wintry Tales of the West, 2002
West River Waltz, 2006
My Father's Horses, 2007
The Night Ol' Flukie Foundered, 2009
Prairie Song, 2013

AWARDS

Will Rogers Medallion Award for Excellence in Cowboy Poetry, *West River Waltz*, 2006

Cowboy, poet, singer, and songwriter D. W. Groethe was born and reared in the badlands of western North Dakota on the family ranch homesteaded by his Norwegian immigrant grandfather in 1903. The family still owns the home quarter. He grew up in a musical family. His grandfather was a church organist, and his father sang and played the fiddle. His mother started him on piano lessons when he was in the second grade, and after high school he played keyboard in several country-folk-rock bands. He also studied theater at the University of North Dakota, a skill he credits with helping him as a stage performer. He learned to play the guitar and started writing songs and poems about life in the West, heeding the advice to "write about what you know." Indeed, his poems and songs reflect his take on the life of a twenty-first-century cowboy. The *Billings Gazette* says, "When he sings, you hear the bawling calves, smell the fire at branding time and shiver at the chill of a skin-strapping prairie wind. You ache at the contradiction of ranch life, starving to death to do the thing you love."[1] In 1991 D. W. pulled up stakes, moved to Bainville, Montana, and started working as a ranch hand. Unlike many cowboys who hate it, he likes fixing fences. He says, "I get out there, I am by myself, I can sit and holler and yodel. It's kind of like learning to fiddle. You gotta be out in the middle of nowhere."[2]

Over the years, D. W. has been invited to perform his eclectic assortment of poems and tunes at the National Cowboy Poetry Gathering, in Elko, Nevada, two National Folk Festivals, the Library of Congress, the Kennedy Center, and a host of other places all over the West. His poems have been featured in *American Cowboy*, *Cowboy*, *Rattle*, *Cowboy Way*,

and *Rope Burns*; on CowboyPoetry.com and on the Western Folklife Center and National Public Radio's *What's in a Song*; in *Ranch Rhymes: Cowboy Poetry and Music from the Western Folklife Center*; and in the *Bar-D Roundup* from the Center for Western and Cowboy Poetry. He has recorded four albums and has written five books of poetry, one of which, *West River Waltz*, won the Will Rogers Medallion Award for Excellence in Cowboy Poetry.

WYLIE GUSTAFSON

Wylie Gustafson grew up on his family's ranch in Conrad, Montana. His father, the legendary "Rib" Gustafson, was one of the first veterinarians in north-central Montana. In addition to being a rancher, roper, and horseman, Rib also played the guitar and sang old-time cowboy songs. Wylie not only learned about horses and cattle from his dad, but he also inherited his love of music, soaking up a lot of those old songs. His dad even taught him how to yodel, a skill that he would become famous for when the Internet company Yahoo! hired Gustafson to yodel the company's trademark "Ya-hooo-ooo!" for its television commercials.

Even though he started out as a child of the rock 'n' roll era, Wylie's love for his western heritage eventually drew him back to western and cowboy music. Wylie is the "real deal," someone who lives the life he sings about. Now, after three decades of writing, recording, and performing, Wylie has matured into a dynamic talent and has become one of the truly authentic voices of the West. One critic called him "the coolest cowpoke around. Forget everything you hate about modern country, this guy is old-school cool without being a tired period piece."[1] While he has roots in his father's old cowboy songs, Wylie brings a new perspective to his music. In a 2001 interview for *Western Horseman* magazine, Wylie said, "I have a huge respect for performers like the Sons of the Pioneers, Marty Robbins, and Gene Autry. We do a lot of those songs in our show but I wanted to take western music in a new direction and create something interesting—something that today's generation can relate to somehow, whether it be my working cowboy friends in Montana or the kids in Seattle."[2]

DISCOGRAPHY

Wylie & the Wild West Show, 1992
Get Wild, 1994
Glory Trail: Cowboy and Traditional Gospel Songs, 1996
Cattle Call: Songs of the Wild West, 1996
Way Out West, 1997
Total Yodel!, 1998
Ridin' the Hi-Line, 2000
Paradise, 2000
Hooves of the Horses, 2004
Cowboy Ballads & Dance Songs, 2004
LIVE! At the Tractor, 2005
Bucking Horse Moon, 2007
Christmas for Cowboys, 2007
Hang-n-Rattle!, 2009
Unwired, 2009
Yodel Boogie!, 2008
Raven on the Wind, 2011
Rocketbuster, 2011
Sky Tones: Songs of Montana, 2012
Relic, 2014
Song of the Horse, 2014

In addition to having a successful career in music, when not touring he still gets up every day and tends to the livestock on his quarter horse ranch near the town of Conrad, Montana. He says it grounds him and is the backbone of his art. As an accomplished cutting horse enthusiast, Wylie has claimed several hard-won regional and national titles within the National Cutting Horse Association while riding his horse, Whiskey. Wylie says, "The connection between my cowboy life and my music is extremely close."

Over the last twenty-five years, Wylie and his band, the Wild West, have performed their cutting-edge amalgam of cowboy, swing, folk, and yodeling music worldwide. They are popular on the festival and theater circuit. They have performed at such prestigious venues as the National Folk Festival, the National Cowboy Poetry Gathering, MerleFest, the Bumbershoot Festival, the Stagecoach Festival, *A Prairie Home Companion*, the *Conan O'Brien Show*, and the Grand Ole Opry (with over fifty guest appearances). Worldwide, Wylie has been a cowboy ambassador, taking western music to China, Russia, Australia, Europe, South America, and Japan. Wylie now has recorded more than twenty nationally distributed albums. He has established himself as western music's premier yodeler and shares his secrets in *How to Yodel: Lessons to Tickle Your Tonsils*. When asked to define his music, Wylie explains, "We are a good-time cowboy band that hates to be boring!"[3]

BOOKS

How to Yodel: Lessons to Tickle Your Tonsils, 2007

AWARDS

Academy of Western Artists, Yodeler of the Year, 2004 and 2005

Western Music Association, Group of the Year, 2005

Western Music Association, Western Swing Album of the Year, *LIVE! At the Tractor* (2006) and *Bucking Horse Moon* (2008)

Academy of Western Artists, Western Swing Duo/Group of the Year, 2008

Western Writers of America, Spur Award for Best Western Song, "Hang-n-Rattle," 2010

KENNY HALL

DISCOGRAPHY

Ridin', 2005

Cowboy singer, poet, and fifth-generation horseman Kenny Hall is a native son of Utah whose great-great-grandparents came west with Brigham Young. His ancestors settled many areas in Utah, including Wellsville and Hyde Park. Kenny lives in the small southern Utah town of Tropic with his wife, Jean, in a rustic homestead where he raises saddle mules, horses, and cattle on land that has been passed down through the generations of Jean's ancestors, the Ott family. Kenny is a former Professional Rodeo Cowboys Association bull rider and racehorse trainer. He builds award-winning custom cowboy camp wagons and is a respected saddlemaker, gear maker, and horseshoer. He has spent most of his life working with cattle, sheep, and horses and helping close friends on their farms and ranches. Kenny's day job is working for Bryce Canyon National Park, where he spends many hours in the saddle, riding the park's red rock canyons. Kenny says of the cowboy life, "It is something I actually live every day of my life. My goal is to pass it on and keep alive the heritage that has been handed down to me."[1]

Kenny started playing music on a tenor guitar he bought with money earned from raising pigs and moved on to mastering the six-string. In his early years Kenny played with a variety of musical groups. Then his heart turned to writing and performing western or cowboy music. He is an accomplished singer, songwriter, and guitarist and has been recognized nationally for his songwriting abilities in the annual American Songwriters Competition. He formed his own Desert Sage Band, has played with the Red Rock Wranglers, and currently performs solo or with his newest group, Latigo. He is a member of the National Western Music Association and the Academy of Western Artists and an active member, board member, and past vice president of the Cowboy Poets of Utah. He performs regularly throughout southern Utah venues such as Western Legends in Kanab, the Butch Cassidy Days in Beaver County, the Everett Ruess Days in Escalante, and many others.[2] He also has performed at the National Cowboy Poetry Gathering in Elko, Nevada.

R. W. HAMPTON

Cowboy singer, songwriter, actor, and playwright R. W. Hampton was born in Houston, Texas, and grew up in town, but he has lived and worked on ranches all over the West. Today R. W. lives with his wife, Lisa, on their Clearview Ranch at the foot of the Sangre de Cristo Mountains near Cimarron, New Mexico. His first job cowboying was as a wrangler at the Philmont Scout Ranch in the mountains near Cimarron. He found the work agreed with him, and he worked at the Philmont for three years and then took a riding job at the Red River Ranch, near Springer, New Mexico. He took a stab at college but found he was more interested in horses and playing his guitar. He left school and went to work for the Spade Ranch in New Mexico. Subsequently he worked for the IL Ranch in northern Nevada, and then went back to Texas and New Mexico and worked for the 4T, the K Cross Ranches, the Quien Sabe, and the LS Ranches. From there he moved north to the ZX Ranch in Oregon and the Pickerel Land and Cattle Company in Wyoming.

In high school R. W. developed an interest in playing guitar and singing cowboy songs in his rich baritone voice, and he continued to do this while cowboying. He wrote songs based on his experiences and played mostly in bunkhouses and at roundup wagons. He began singing in public and found many of the singing jobs paid much better than his cowboy wages of $800 a month. Soon he was performing at cowboy poetry gatherings, rodeos, churches, and private functions.

In 1985 R. W. worked in the Kenny Rogers film *Wild Horses*. He has appeared in twelve movies since then, including *The Tracker*, with Kris Kristofferson, and two other Kenny Rogers films. He has performed all over the United States and was a special guest at the 2010 British Country Music Awards in London; he also has performed in Australia and Brazil.

DISCOGRAPHY

Ridin' the Dreamland Range, 1996
Then Sings My Soul, 1998
The Last Cowboy, 1999
Always in My Heart, 2001
Troubadour, 2003
Our First Noel, 2005
I Believe, 2005
Oklahoma . . . Where the West Remains!, 2007
My Old Friends, 2008
Austin to Boston, 2010
My Country's Not For Sale, 2013
Hell in a Helmet, 2013
This Cowboy, 2014

R. W. has received numerous awards and accolades, including induction into the Western Music Association's Hall of Fame in 2011. In 1993 R. W. and his brother Jeff, along with playwright David Marquis, wrote a one-man stage play, *The Last Cowboy*, set in 2025, in which an aging cowboy recounts the history of the cowboy through monologue and song. *The Last Cowboy—His Journey*, an album inspired by the play, earned R. W. his first Wrangler Award in 2000 for Excellence in Dramatic Presentation and Original Music Compositions from the National Cowboy and Western Heritage Museum.

AWARDS

Academy of Western Artists' first Will Rogers Award for Male Vocalist of the Year and Entertainer of the Year, 1996

Academy of Western Artists, Western Music Album of the Year, *Ridin' the Dreamland Range*, 1997

National Cowboy and Western Heritage Museum, Wrangler Award for Excellence in Dramatic Presentation and Original Music Compositions, *The Last Cowboy—His Journey*, 2000

Academy of Western Artists, Western Music Male Vocalist of the Year, 1999, 2002, and 2006

Western Music Association, Male Performer of the Year, 2004 and 2010

Western Music Association, Song of the Year, "For the Freedom," 2006

Inducted into Western Music Association Hall of Fame, 2011

JONI HARMS

Joni Harms grew up on a ranch in Oregon that was homesteaded by her great-great-grandfather in 1872. She still lives and works on the ranch with her husband, Jeff, and their two children, Olivia and Luke, raising beef cattle, sheep, and Christmas trees. Joni has been singing since age four, when she first entertained guests at her aunt's hotel with "I Want to Be a Cowboy's Sweetheart." By the time she was in her teens she was writing her own songs, combining an interest in singing with the life of a ranch kid. In high school she won a talent contest sponsored by the Future Farmers of America that launched her on her musical career. As a teenage rodeo queen, she performed on the rodeo circuit, frequently singing the national anthem.

She later began taking trips to Nashville in search of a recording contract. She signed to record for the Universal label, a co-venture with MCA Records, and reached the country top forty in April 1989 with the single, "I Need a Wife." The follow-up single, "The Only Thing Bluer Than His Eyes," reached the country charts in June. Joni moved to Capitol Records in 1990, and there released *Hometown Girl*, which did not chart. During the 1990s she pursued her musical career while marrying, raising two children, and continuing to live and work on her family ranch. She followed *Hometown Girl* with *Whatever It Takes* and an all-original album, *Christmas in the Country*. By 1998 she had changed record companies again, moving to Warner Bros. Records, which released *Cowgirl Dreams*. In 1999 Joni made a children's album, *Are We There Yet?*, accompanied by a coloring book. Based on a song from that album, she also wrote and published the children's books *Stan and Bert* and *The Little Grey Donkey*. In the fall of 2001 she released a new country album, *After All*, on her Real West Productions label through the independent record company

DISCOGRAPHY
Singles
"I Need a Wife," 1989
"The Only Thing Bluer Than His Eyes," 1989

Albums
Thoughts of You, 1985
I Want to Sing for You, 1986
Hometown Girl, 1990
Whatever It Takes, 1995
Christmas in the Country, 1996
Cowgirl Dreams, 1998
Are We There Yet?, 1999
After All, 2001
Let's Put the Western Back in the Country, 2004
That's Faith, 2006
Harms Way, 2011
Oregon to Ireland, 2014

Paras Recordings. After her stint in the country music world of Nashville, Joni gravitated back toward her western roots and has become a favorite on the festival circuit and the western music scene, though she will go east for performances on the Grand Ole Opry and at Carnegie Hall.

Joni says on her website, "I personally can't live without Western music. I like a lot of today's country music, but the truth of the matter is that I'm very serious about keeping the western side of country music alive. The majority of my songs include lyrics of the west, because I love to write about things I've experienced. Rodeo, cowboys, and the ranch way of living shows through a lot in my music." Joni adds, "I always want the songs I sing to be a good representation of who I am."[1]

AWARDS

Academy of Western Artists, Rising Star of the Year, 1999
Academy of Western Artists, Western Music Female Vocalist of the Year, 2001
Academy of Western Artists, Entertainer of the Year, 2002
Western Music Association, Female Vocalist of the Year and Song of the Year, "Cowboy Up," 2003
Academy of Western Artists, Western Music Album of the Year, *Let's Put the Western Back in the Country*, 2004
Academy of Western Artists, Western Swing Female Vocalist of the Year, 2011

Joni working cattle on her ranch

KRISTYN HARRIS

DISCOGRAPHY

My Mustang, My Martin, and Me, 2010
Let Me Ride, 2013
Badger and the Belles (with Rich O'Brien and Devon Dawson), 2014
Down the Trail, 2015

Kristyn Harris is a young western and western swing performer from McKinney, Texas. Born in 1994, the diminutive singer is noted for her powerful vocals, sock rhythm guitar playing, songwriting, and outstanding yodeling. In 2014 she became the youngest person ever to win the Western Music Association Female Performer of the Year, and she was also awarded the 2013 Academy of Western Artists Western Music Female Vocalist of the Year. Kristyn started playing when she was fourteen years

Kristyn riding Tacky

old, honing her swing guitar skills and infusing her lyrics and melodies with the ranching-inspired themes that make up western swing and cowboy music. An accomplished horsewoman, Kristyn starts horses, an activity she loves as much as making music. She adopted and trained two mustangs. She spent several years in 4-H, and she brought home the National Hippology ("Study of the Horse") Championship with her 4-H team in 2010.[1] She has a sincere devotion to the land and livestock, and her horse experiences are frequently reflected in her songs.

In 2015 Kristyn was honored by Cowtown Society of Western Swing as Rising Star of the Year. She received the 2013 Cowboy Swing Album of the Year award for *Let Me Ride*, the 2012 Crescendo Award, and the 2012 Female Yodeler of the Year from the Western Music Association. She has performed on national television as part of RFD-TV's *The e-Penny Gilley Show* and *The Shotgun Red Variety Show*, and on Nickelodeon's game show *Figure It Out*, and she is featured in a number of western documentaries, including a film that aired in four European countries in 2014.[2] She regularly tours the western United States.

DON HEDGPETH

Don Hedgpeth, a fifth-generation Texan, was born in Seagrave and grew up in Banquete. The family moved to South Texas during the long drought of the 1950s, where he learned about cowboying from Mexican vaqueros south of the Nueces River working cross-bred Brahma cattle. He got his first job for cowboy wages at fourteen, doctoring screwworms in the brush country. Don competed in high school rodeo and continued to ride bareback broncs and bulls while pursuing a degree from Texas A&M. After graduating he went to Montana to work as a cowboy and dude wrangler.[1] His father played guitar and sang cowboy songs, so Don grew up around the old songs and knew the words to them, but he didn't play the guitar until 1964. That year Don was at a rodeo in Uvalde, Texas, with some friends, one of whom was leaving a job wrangling dudes in Montana, and Don thought that sounded like a god gig. They called the guy's boss in Montana, and he had two questions: Could Don shoe horses and could he play the guitar and sing? Don said yes, went out and bought a guitar, and learned three chords, and in thirty days he was campfire ready. Don

modestly says, "That's where my musical talent plateaued and where it's been ever since,"[2] but he has been a featured performer at a number of cowboy events around the West, including the National Cowboy Poetry Gathering in Elko, Nevada, and the Texas Cowboy Poetry Gathering in Alpine. He has also written some fine cowboy poetry, such as his poem "For Them That Tend to Lonesome," which was put to music by western singer Don Edwards.

While living in Montana Don met his wife, Sug, and they later returned to Texas, where Don taught history. He has worked for the National Cowboy and Western Heritage Museum in Oklahoma City, the Buffalo Bill Center of the West in Cody, Wyoming, and the Texas Cattleman's Association. Don is the founding editor of *Persimmon Hill*, the journal of the National Cowboy and Western Heritage Museum, and the author or coauthor of more than a dozen books on western history, cowboys, and western art. Today Don and Sug live near Medina, Texas.

BOOKS

Spurs Were a-Jinglin': A Brief Look at the Wyoming Range Country, 1975
Bettina: Portraying Life in Art, illustrated by Bettina Steinke, 1978
The Texas Breed: A Cowboy Anthology, 1978
Cowboy Artist: The Joe Beeler Story, illustrated by Joe Beeler, 1979
From Broncs to Bronzes: The Life and Work of Grant Speed, 1979
They Rode Good Horses: The First 50 Years of the American Quarter Horse Association, 1990
The Art of Tom Lovell, An Invitation to History, coauthored by Walt Reed, 1993
Howard Terpning: Spirit of the Plains People, coauthored by Howard Terpning, 2001
The Fence That Me and Shorty Built (foreword), by Red Steagall, 2001
Under Western Skies: The Art of Bob Pummill (foreword), by Michael Duty, 2003
Desert Dreams: The Western Art of Don Crowley, illustrated by Don Crowley, 2003
The Story of Leanin' Tree: Art and Enterprise in the American West, 2008
Follow the Sun: Robert Lougheed, 2010

AWARDS

Heritage Award, Texas Cowboy Poetry Gathering, 2002

Mike on Ryder in the Tetons

MICHAEL HURWITZ

Michael Hurwitz was born in Laramie, Wyoming, and has high plains roots going back four generations. He started cowboying at an early age: haying, branding cattle, fixing fence, and logging lots of saddle time. He has worked as a cowboy, broncbuster, hunting guide, dude wrangler, carpenter, surveyor, and, for the past thirty years, as a musician. He got his first guitar at thirteen. He remembers, "It was a brown one, with the strings a half-inch off the neck. I played till my fingers bled and the dogs ran away from home never to return."

Mike learned old cowboy songs from his dad and country blues from his Mississippi-born mother. He listened to the greats of the period—Hank Williams, Muddy Waters, Johnny Horton, Jimmy Rodgers—and eventually started writing songs himself, blending the influences into what he calls "prairie blues." After getting an electric guitar he started playing weekends in local honky-tonks with a country band, and occasionally still plays with those old friends. Today he lives in Alta, Wyoming, by the Tetons, performing solo and with his band, the Aimless Drifters, which includes pedal steel, piano, accordion, mandolin, fiddle, harp, bass, and drums.

Perhaps Jerome Clark, in *Rambles Magazine*, sums Mike up best: "Nothing of the drugstore-cowboy Nashville hat act, singer/guitarist Michael Hurwitz is a man with bonafide range credentials. These days, working the circuit from his home on the Wyoming/Idaho border, he and his band, the Aimless Drifters, preserve the unadulterated Western sounds in clubs, bars, and dance halls far from the madding crowds. His music is plain-spoken and straightforward, sung in a charmingly cracked baritone, the voice of a man who's been around and has a supply of good stories—funny, rueful or grim—to pass on."[1]

KEN JONES

DISCOGRAPHY

Meanwhile, Back at the Ranch
   (cassette), 1987
Family Tree, 1995

Ken Jones was born in 1951 in Amarillo, Texas, where his father had relocated during World War II, after growing up on a ranch outside of Thermopolis, Wyoming. In 1957 his father took a job with the Hualapai Indians, managing their trading post and tribal cattle herd in Peach Springs, Arizona.

Ken started riding when he was three or four, and at Peach Springs he began cowboying with the Indians who worked for his father. They ran cattle on most of the one-million-acre reservation. Ken recalls, "Every weekend I was riding, hunting down wild cattle, or chasing wild horses with the Indian cowboys on the reservation."[1]

Ken's interest in music was sparked when he saw the Beatles on the *Ed Sullivan Show* in 1964. On the reservation he had two Indian friends who also wanted to play, and they started a band called the Weeds, which, Ken points out, was long before "weed."

While they were still living on the reservation, Ken's father bought his uncle's ranch in Big Timber, Montana. Ken spent his summers there and worked for the nearby Cremer Ranch in Melville, Montana, from age thirteen through high school. After ten years on the reservation, the family moved to the Big Timber ranch. Following high school graduation, Ken attended the University of Montana at Missoula, and while he was in college developed an interest in writing songs. He did summer work at the Triangle X Ranch up the South Fork of the Shoshone River out of Cody, Wyoming, the same guest ranch his father had wrangled at thirty years before. It was there that Ken began playing cowboy music at the ranch's campfires. He continued dude wrangling throughout college at the same ranch. After graduating from college Ken worked for the Highland Livestock Company in Livingston, Montana, for a year, but

he missed the dude wrangling, the fun, and the music. He took a job managing the old Valley Ranch, at the end of the South Fork, back in Cody, one of the oldest dude ranches in the country, started in 1914. After he had been there for three years, a couple who were regular guests mentioned their interest in buying a dude ranch and offered him equity in the place for managing it. After searching for a place, they finally decided to build their own ranch. This is the famous Home Ranch, eighteen miles north of Steamboat, in Clark, Colorado.

Inspired by the western group Riders in the Sky and their stage show, combining music with comedy, Ken decided to start doing stage shows for guests at the ranch. He converted an old Colorado-style barn on the ranch into a performance area with a stage. Ken started hiring wranglers who could play music. He says, "I went for the good ones, the ones who were light years better than me."[2] This was the beginning of the Ranch Hand Band. They played together for twenty years. During Ken's twenty-eight years at the Home Ranch, they did more than two thousand stage and campfire shows.

After retiring from the Home Ranch in 2005, Ken and his wife, Nancy, moved to the Flathead Valley in Montana, where he pursued a lifelong dream of being a saddlemaker and leatherworker. He has a saddle shop on their place, and between that and his other passion, cowboy mounted shooting, he keeps very busy. Ken says, "I continue to pursue horsemanship and go to brandings whenever possible, along with saddle making, mounted shooting, and playing music around any campfire I can find."[3]

WALT LARUE

AWARDS
The Motion Picture and Television Fund, Golden Boot Award, 2007

Cowboy, movie stuntman, artist, amateur boxer, and singer Walt LaRue was born in 1918, either in Fall River, Massachusetts, or in Canada, depending on your source, to American parents. He had relatives who had horses, and Walt learned to ride and break horses. He spent part of his early life as a guide and packer in Glacier National Park and also in Yosemite and the High Sierras of California. That horseback work led to rodeoing, and Walt spent part of the next twelve years of his life traveling to rodeos, riding bareback horses and bulls. In 1942 he joined the Cowboy's Turtle Association, the forerunner of the Rodeo Cowboys Association, which eventually became the Professional Rodeo Cowboys Association, of which he was a gold card member.[1]

Rodeoing eventually led Walt to a career as a Hollywood stuntman. He was lucky to be part of that business during the 1940s and 1950s, Hollywood's golden age of westerns. Walt said, "I was ridin' buckin' horses . . . drivin' wagons . . . doin' falls . . . stuff like that."[2] He appeared in dozens of movies and television shows, mostly, but not all, westerns, stretching over a long career, beginning with *Lightning Carson Strikes Again* in 1938, and including roles in such notable films as *It's a Mad, Mad, Mad, Mad World* (1963), *Blazing Saddles* (1974), *The Blues Brothers* (1980), *Pale Rider* (1985), and *Back to the Future Part III* (1990).[3]

Walt was a natural entertainer and storyteller. "I sang everywhere, but I didn't play. Then I see some little kid somewhere playin' the guitar . . . playin' the hell out of it! And I figured . . . if he can learn to play it, I guess I can. So I bought this guitar from the bartender . . . and in a couple years, I played pretty good."[4] He played local clubs, entertained his friends, and sang his old-time cowboy songs for his fellow actors

and crews on movie shoots. He also wrote some fine songs, including "Pretty Pauline," which was recorded by Buck Ramsey, Skip Gorman, Dave Stamey, and others. Walt was always a fine artist, his lifetime of cartoons, sketches, drawings, and paintings numbering in the thousands. His greatest influences were the works of Charlie Russell and Will James, and evidence of both can be seen in Walt's work. Walt did drawings and paintings commercially for Levi Strauss, Weber Bread, Blevins Buckles, Paul Bond Boots, and other businesses, and from 1945 to 1952 Walt drew cartoon covers for the *Buckboard*, the official magazine of the Rodeo Cowboys Association. His paintings, all westerns, are in private collections, galleries, and museums all over the world. Walt passed away on June 12, 2010, at the age of ninety-one.

CHRIS LEDOUX

Chris LeDoux, "the Singing Bronc Rider," was born in Biloxi, Mississippi. His father was in the US Air Force, and the family moved frequently. He began riding horses while visiting his grandparents on their farm in Michigan.[1] Chris first tried his hand at rodeo at age thirteen, in Denison, Texas, and was soon winning junior rodeo competitions. He had decided on competitive rodeo riding as a career by the age of fourteen, and he competed in rodeo events throughout his high school years. When his family relocated to Cheyenne, Wyoming, Chris attended Cheyenne Central High School and twice won the Wyoming State Rodeo Championship bareback riding title. He was awarded a rodeo scholarship to Casper College in Casper, Wyoming. It was during this time he started playing guitar and writing songs. While a student at Eastern New Mexico University (to which he had transferred as a junior), Chris won the Intercollegiate National Bareback Riding Championship.[2]

In 1970 Chris turned professional, competing on the national rodeo circuit in some eighty rodeos a year. Meanwhile, he started writing songs about rodeo life, and in two years, he had enough songs to make up an album and recorded them in a friend's basement. He soon established a recording company, American Cowboy Songs, with his father, and started selling his albums out of the back of his truck at rodeos. He called his music a combination of western soul, sagebrush blues, cowboy folk, and rodeo rock 'n' roll. In 1976 Chris won the world bareback riding championship at the National Finals Rodeo in Oklahoma City.[3] He retired in 1980 due to injuries and to spend more time with his family.

DISCOGRAPHY

Songs of Rodeo Life, 1971
Rodeo Songs "Old and New," 1973
Songs of Rodeo and Country, 1974
Rodeo and Living Free, 1975
Life as a Rodeo Man, 1975
Songbook of the American West, 1976
Sing Me a Song, Mr. Rodeo Man, 1977
Cowboys Ain't Easy to Love, 1978
Paint Me Back Home in Wyoming, 1978
Western Tunesmith, 1979
Old Cowboy Heroes, 1980
Sounds of the Western Country, 1980
He Rides Wild Horses, 1981
Used to Want to Be a Cowboy, 1982
Old Cowboy Classics, 1983
Thirty Dollar Cowboy, 1983
Melodies and Memories, 1984
Wild and Wooly, 1986
Gold Buckle Dreams, 1987
Chris LeDoux and the Saddle Boogie Band, 1988
Powder River, 1989
Radio and Rodeo Hits, 1990

Concert at the Dee Events
Center, Weber State University,
Weber, Utah 1997

With his rodeo career ended, Chris settled on a ranch in Kaycee, Wyoming, with his family. He could now focus all his attention on his music, writing and recording his songs. He also began playing concerts. By 1982 he had sold over 250,000 copies of his albums, with little or no marketing. By the end of the decade, he had self-released twenty-two albums.[4] Chris chose not to sign a recording contract with a major label, deciding instead to maintain his independence and control over his work. In 1989, however, he suddenly attained national attention when Garth Brooks mentioned listening to "a worn-out tape of Chris LeDoux" in the song "Much Too Young (to Feel This Damn Old)."[5] This led to Chris signing a contract with Liberty Records, and he released his first national album, *Western Underground*, in 1991. His follow-up album, *Whatcha Gonna Do with a Cowboy*, went gold and reached the top ten on country music charts in the United States and Canada. For the next decade Chris continued to record for Liberty. He released six additional records. Toward the end of his career, Chris began recording songs written by other artists, which he attributed to the challenge of composing new lyrics. In 2000 he released *Cowboy*, in which he returned to his roots, re-recording many of his earliest songs.

Chris passed away in March 2005, following a battle with a rare form of cancer.[6] Later that same year he was one of six former rodeo cowboys to be inducted into the ProRodeo Hall of Fame in Colorado Springs. He was the first person ever inducted in two categories, for his bareback riding and in the "notables" category for his contributions to the sport through music.[7] The town of Kaycee, Wyoming, erected a larger-than-life-size sculpture of Chris depicting his 1976 world championship ride on Stormy Weather.[8]

DISCOGRAPHY (continued)

Western Underground, 1991
Whatcha Gonna Do with a Cowboy, 1992
Under This Old Hat, 1993
Haywire, 1994
Best of Chris LeDoux, 1994
American Cowboy, 1994
Rodeo Rock and Roll Collection, 1995
Stampede, 1996
Live, 1997
One Road Man, 1998
20 Greatest Hits, 1999
Cowboy, 2000
After the Storm, 2002
The Capitol Collection (1990–2000), 2002
Horsepower, 2003
Twenty Originals: The Early Years, 2004
Anthology, Volume 1, 2005
The Ultimate Collection, 2006
Classic Chris LeDoux, 2008

AWARDS

Inducted into ProRodeo Hall of Fame, 2005
Academy of Country Music Pioneer Award, 2005

DARON LITTLE

AWARDS

Academy of Western Artists,
    Western Music Male
    Vocalist of the Year, 2009

Daron Little has cowboyed in Colorado, Nebraska, and Montana and now lives and cowboys full time at the headquarters division of the Silver Spur Ranch in Encampment, Wyoming. He and his wife raise their three daughters there and are at home on the ranch.[1] He describes himself as a "bovine relocation engineer and cowpunch music guitar picker/singer." Daron doesn't consider himself a "cowboy singer," but a working ranch cowboy who also happens to be a singer-songwriter. "I am a picker and grinner and roper and rider, but mostly I just try to be a good dad," he has said on Facebook. He writes songs from a cowboy's point of view and hopes that all who appreciate and value the western lifestyle can enjoy them. According to one online profile, Daron believes that to write cowboy music, you have to live it. Otherwise it is romance and not reality.[2] Singer and songwriter Juni Fisher says of Daron, "If Bob Dylan decided he wanted to be a cowboy, and write songs about his lifestyle, one would wonder if he would seek out Daron Little to show him the way."[3] Daron was the 2009 Academy of Western Artists Western Music Male Vocalist of the Year and was a finalist for the 2010 Western Writers of America Spur Award for Best Western Song. His first release, *The Faraway Look*, became a top ten album on the western music charts, and his second release, *Ranch Cowboy Music*, also met with critical acclaim.

Daron's musical influences include Dave Stamey, Mike Beck, Jack Johnson, Muddy Waters, Chris LeDoux, Ian Tyson, and even Bob Marley. Daron has performed at numerous cowboy poetry gatherings, including the Poetry Gathering and Buckaroo Fair in Heber City, Utah, and other events such as the Western Heritage Classic Ranch Rodeo and Trade Show in Abilene, Texas; the Working Ranch Cowboy's Association Ranch Rodeo World Finals in Amarillo, Texas; and the Annual Grand Encampment Cowboy Gathering in Encampment, Wyoming.

CORB LUND

Singer and songwriter Corb Lund was born in Taber, Alberta, Canada, and grew up on a rural ranch in southern Alberta, the fourth generation of ranchers and cowboys. "My family is all ranchers and rodeo people," Lund says. "They've been in Canada for about 100 years, and before that they were raising cattle in Utah and Nevada. Some of my relatives are still down there. I grew up rodeoing. I was a steer rider—that's like the junior version of bull riding. I was on horseback pretty much as soon as I could walk."[1]

Music was an important part of his early life. Lund says, "My grandpas used to sing all these old western cowboy ballads. Those songs come from before recorded music—they're traditional numbers that the cowboys always sing in camp, or just for fun, to entertain themselves. My grandpas knew all those songs. The first song I ever knew was 'The Strawberry Roan.'"[2] Lund eventually left the ranch and moved to Edmonton, where he enrolled in Grant MacEwan College to pursue a musical education. He spent a decade playing indie rock music before gravitating back toward his western roots in the early 1990s. Since then he has gone on to become one of Canada's foremost "country" singers, releasing nine albums and racking up an impressive array of awards. He and his band, the Hurtin' Albertans, have become popular performers at events such as the Calgary Stampede and the National Cowboy Poetry Gathering in Elko, Nevada.

Corb at National Cowboy Poetry Gathering, Elko, Nevada

AWARDS

Canadian Folk Music Awards
English Songwriter of the Year, 2008

Edmonton Music Awards (Canada)
Male Artist of the Year, 2013
Country Recording of the Year, *Cabin Fever*, 2013
People's Choice Award, 2013

French Association of Country Music (France)
Independent Artist of the Year, 2005 and 2006

Indie Acoustic Project
Best Lyrics, *Horse Soldier! Horse Soldier!*, 2007

The Indies (Canadian Independent Music Awards)
Favourite Folk Artist/Group, 2006 and 2008
Favourite Country Artist, Group or Duo of the Year, 2007

Juno Awards (Canada)
Independent Group or Duo of the Year, 2004 and 2005
Roots and Traditional Album of the Year (Solo), *Hair in My Eyes Like a Highland Steer*, 2006
Roots Artist or Group of the Year, 2004, 2005, 2006, 2007, 2008, 2009, 2010, and 2013

Western Canadian Music Awards
Outstanding Album (Independent), *Five Dollar Bill*, 2003
Entertainer of the Year, 2005
Songwriter of the Year, 2006
Outstanding Independent Recording, *Hair in My Eyes Like a Highland Steer*, 2006
Outstanding Roots Recording, *Hair in My Eyes Like a Highland Steer* (2006) and *Horse Soldier! Horse Soldier!* (2008)

GARY MCMAHAN

Singer, songwriter, poet, humorist, and yodeler Gary McMahan is a native of Greeley, Colorado. Ramblin' Jack Elliott has called Gary "the King of the Cowboy Singers." Chris LeDoux called him "our cowboy Bob Dylan." He is one of a handful of cowboy singers who was already active before the cowboy poetry gathering movement. He says, "I can remember when Ian Tyson, Chris LeDoux, and I were the only genuine cowboy types kicking around Nashville in the early seventies. All three of us were pretty much out of work, and it stayed that way for over a decade. But we all three hung and rattled and made it through that drought. I managed to extract myself from horse outfits and singing in windy little Naugahyde bars when the cowboy poetry gatherings came along."[1]

Gary grew up hauling cattle with his father from Montana and the Dakotas to Texas and all points in between. He has done everything from cowboying to guiding. He can brand, rope, ride broncs, fence, hay, shoe horses, pack, and drive teams. After spending two years studying animal science at Colorado State University, he made the decision to become a cowboy songwriter, incorporating his experiences into his music.

In the early 1970s he moved to Nashville, but after five years there, he moved back to Colorado. While living in Nashville he was signed by New York–based Tomato Records. At the time, that label had only three other artists: Dick Gregory, Townes Van Zandt, and Philip Glass.

McMahan has written more than three hundred songs and poems and has recorded six albums. His songs have been recorded by artists

DISCOGRAPHY

Colorado Blue, 1978
Saddle 'em Up and Go, 1988
A Cowboyin' Day, 1992
Poems and Yodels, 1997
Gary McMahan: Live in Elko, Nevada, 2006
Goin' My Way?, 2009

BOOKS

Gary McMahan in Poetry and Song, 1997

AWARDS

Western Music Association, National Champion Yodeler, 1991
National Cowboy and Western Heritage Museum, Wrangler Award for Outstanding Original Western Composition, "The First Cowboy Song," 1993

such as Chris LeDoux, Ian Tyson, and Riders in the Sky. His performing career got a boost when he was invited to perform at the first National Cowboy Poetry Gathering in Elko, Nevada, in 1985, where he was well received. Cowboy poet Baxter Black encouraged him to do more of it.[2] *Western Horseman* magazine included his song "The Old Double Diamond" as one of the top thirteen cowboy songs of all time.

Today Gary lives in Bellevue, Colorado, and does sixty to eighty dates a year, mostly at banquets, concerts, and events such as the National Cowboy Poetry Gathering and the Colorado Cowboy Gathering, which he cofounded in 1988. The Western Music Association named him National Champion Yodeler in 1991, and he is often called on to teach yodeling workshops. In a 2014 interview in *Western Way* magazine, McMahan said, "I've made my living with either a horse or guitar or both for the last forty years, and it's been a great life."[3]

Gary driving Pete and Pat

CHUCK MILNER

DISCOGRAPHY

Range Partners (with R. W.
    Hampton, Donnie Cates,
    and Emily Winters), 1998
Cowboy Days, 2000
Trails Less Traveled, 2008

AWARDS

Heritage Award, Texas
    Cowboy Poetry
    Gathering, 2005

Chuck Milner is a singer-songwriter from Oklahoma who has been playing cowboy music for twenty-five years. He has spent most of his adult life around cattle and horses. Working on ranches since college provided Chuck with the firsthand experience to sing about a cowboy's way of life. He has been a featured performer at the John F. Kennedy Center for the Performing Arts; the Smithsonian Folklife Festival; the National Cowboy Poetry Gathering in Elko, Nevada; the Texas Cowboy Poetry Gathering in Alpine; the Lowell Folk Music Festival in Lowell, Massachusetts; the National Cutting Horse Association Futurity Finals in Fort Worth, Texas; the Working Ranch Cowboys Association Rodeo Finals in Amarillo, Texas; and the Rafter S Roping in Cyril, Oklahoma. For twenty-two years he has performed at the Chuck Wagon Gathering at the National Cowboy and Western Heritage Museum in Oklahoma City. He is a former artist-in-residence for the Oklahoma State Arts Council and has also worked with the Mid-America Arts Council and the National Council for the Traditional Arts.[1]

He and his wife, Beth, are raising their two children, Hallie and Cody, on the Rush Creek Ranch in far western Oklahoma, near Reydon, where they run a cow-calf operation, raising Angus cattle and training horses. Their children are fifth-generation ranchers, Beth's family having operated in Greer County, Oklahoma, since 1901. Hallie and Cody often help their dad with his music. Hallie plays the fiddle and Cody plays the mandolin, and with Chuck they perform as the Rush Creek Wranglers.[2]

In 2003 the Milners received a Centennial Ranch Award for their Smoot-Hood Ranch in Greer County. In 2005 Chuck was honored with the Heritage Award by the Texas Cowboy Poetry Gathering.

Sorting dry cows at the MCross ranch

MICHAEL AND DAWN MOON

DISCOGRAPHY

Land of the Columbine, 2004
A Place of Our Own, 2011

Singing and songwriting duo Michael and Dawn Moon live in Clark, Colorado, where Michael is operations manager for the famous Home Ranch. Michael has been writing music since he was a teenager and most often performs with his guitar, though he also plays piano and banjo. Dawn's instrument throughout her life has been her voice. They perform Michael's original songs, as well as some of the classics of western music and other genres.

Michael grew up visiting and helping his grandparents on their ranch in northeastern New Mexico. Dawn grew up outside of Cleveland. After college they met when they both found themselves on the Home Ranch. Michael moved on to a cattle ranch in Clark, Colorado, and they got married. They joined the Peace Corps and served in Ecuador until they found out they were expecting their first child. The couple returned to Colorado, moving to the Spring Creek Ranch south of Kremmling, where they spent the next six years and had two more children as the ranch transitioned from a single-family-owned ranch to Shadow Creek Ranch. In the spring of 2003, Michael took a job on the Nature Conservancy's Matador Ranch grass bank south of Malta, Montana, where he worked with a group of successful neighboring ranchers and learned a lot by seeing each one's different approach. In December of 2004 the couple followed Michael's ranching roots back to New Mexico and Michael worked for the Quivria Coalition on its Valle Grande Ranch grass bank. In 2007 they moved again, to the 88,000-acre Chico Basin Ranch southeast of Colorado Springs, and their growing family was immersed in a ranching culture that included managing cattle horseback with long days in the saddle, branding camps, and hard work. In 2015 they returned to the Home Ranch and Michael became operations manager.

Along with their ranch work, they continued to write and perform music. The duo has played at cowboy poetry gatherings, including the National Cowboy Poetry Gathering, the Texas Cowboy Poetry Gathering, and other events, but they say some of their favorite times have been around a campfire or in a friend's living room.

ROOSTER MORRIS

Writer, musician, and songwriter David Lee Morris was born in Ridgecrest, California, in 1955, and soon acquired the nickname "Rooster." He comes from generations of cowboys. At the age of five, he began riding horses and working cattle with his father on ranches in the tri-state area of Texas, New Mexico, and Oklahoma. Growing up in these remote places, Rooster developed a unique way of entertaining himself. First he started imitating birdcalls and coyote howls, and then he began working on voices.[1] Rooster's musical skills are self-taught as well. He began learning to play the fiddle when he was sixteen, listening to the tunes played by old cowboy fiddlers in the bunkhouses on the ranches where they worked.[2] He also taught himself how to play guitar, mandolin, and bass. By the time he graduated from high school, he was playing for the historic Western Cowpunchers Association in Amarillo, Texas.[3]

For a number of years, Rooster was the manager of the Spring Creek Ranch outside of Dalhart, Texas, on some of the land that was originally part of the legendary XIT Ranch. Rooster's great-uncle, Jess Morris, himself a well-known fiddler, worked on the XIT many years earlier and was recorded by folklorist John Lomax in 1942 on one of his field recording trips. Jess is best known for his arrangement of "Ridin' Ol' Paint," a song he learned from Charlie Willis, a black cowboy who had learned the song on a cattle drive in 1871. Jess eventually crafted his own haunting rendition of the song with his fiddle accompaniment. Rooster now brings things full circle, playing his great-uncle's version. In 1996 cowboy poet and musician Buck Ramsey convinced Rooster to attend the National

DISCOGRAPHY

The Picnic Tree, 1998
Ridin' Ol Paint: Documenting the Canadian River Breaks Fiddle Tradition (compilation), 2000

Cowboy Poetry Gathering in Elko, Nevada, and play fiddle for him during his performances; Rooster has since performed again there and also at other events, such as the Nara Visa Cowboy Gathering in New Mexico. Rooster started writing his own songs in 1997.

In 2000 Rooster retired from ranching and began working with elementary educators all over the nation in children's reading programs. He has traveled extensively to entertain kids and to help them understand how reading can be fun. Eventually, he began writing children's books himself. The first of his successful series of Axle Galench books, for readers in the third grade and up, *Axle Galench and the Gate of No Return*, was released in 2004. Rooster has now performed across the nation for more than four million children in elementary schools, museums, and libraries. He lives in Rockdale, Texas, with his wife, Jody Logsdon.

GLENN OHRLIN

DISCOGRAPHY

The Hell-Bound Train, 1964
*Glenn Ohrlin: Cowboy
    Songs*, 1974
*Just Something My Uncle Told
    Me: Blaggardy Folk Songs
    from the Southern United
    States* (compilation), 1981
Wild Buckaroo, 1983
A Cowboy's Life, 1998
*The Cowboy Tour: A National
    Tour of Cowboy Songs,
    Poetry, Big Windy Stories,
    Humor, and Fiddling*
    (compilation), 2000

BOOKS

*The Hell-Bound Train: A
    Cowboy Songbook*, 1974

AWARDS

National Endowment for the
    Arts, National Heritage
    Fellowship, 1985

Glenn Ohrlin was born in Minneapolis, Minnesota, in 1926 to Swedish and Norwegian parents. He spent his childhood summers at his grandparents' farm in northern Minnesota, where he developed his love of horses and of cowboy music. "In Minnesota, where I was born, everyone sang cowboy songs, even my aunts and uncles," Glenn recalled. "My father was musical; my mother wasn't, particularly. I used to listen to the radio a lot. When I was growing up in the 1930s, every reasonably big radio station had its own singing cowboy. In those days, it wasn't too hard to find one. If a station wanted a cowboy singer, they'd go out and find a working cowboy who knew a few songs." Glenn started singing when he was five and learned to play the guitar when he was about ten years old. "My mother's folks always had a lot of horses," he said. "They used to trail broncs from Montana and North Dakota and sell them to the farmers. And even when I was a little boy, I was fascinated by the horses. I've never been too interested in anything else in my whole life."[1]

When he was fourteen the family moved to California. Two years later Glenn left home to become a working buckaroo in Nevada. During 1943 and 1944 he cowboyed on ranches in Nevada, Arizona, Montana, Wyoming, and California. In 1943 he went to the rodeo in Caliente, Nevada, where he started riding bareback broncs. Glenn continued to compete in bareback and saddle bronc riding until 1963.

In the 1960s he started to perform on the folk music revival circuit. He recorded his first album, *The Hell-Bound Train*, in 1964. During his years as a working cowboy and on the rodeo circuit he acquired an extensive repertory of traditional cowboy songs. In 1974 he published *The Hell-Bound Train: A Cowboy Songbook* with the University of Illinois

Press; it included one hundred of his favorite cowboy songs and became a classic.

That same year, Glenn recorded his second album, *Glenn Ohrlin: Cowboy Songs*, for Philo Records. Glenn also had a great repertoire of bawdy cowboy songs, and in 1981 he was one of a number of artists enlisted to record such songs for a special Rounder LP, *Just Something My Uncle Told Me: Blaggardy Folk Songs from the Southern United States*, which has become a cult classic. In 1983 Glenn recorded an entire album for the Rounder label, *Wild Buckaroo*. In 1983 and 1984 he was the host of and a performer for two pioneering tours produced by the National Council for the Traditional Arts, the Old Puncher's Reunion/Cowboy Tour. He was one of eight working cowboys, from Hawaii to Louisiana, who traveled over thirty thousand miles by road in the western United States and Hawaii, bringing tall tales, fiddling, songs, jokes, and cowboy poetry to small towns with ranching traditions.[2]

In 1985 Glenn became the first cowboy to receive a prestigious National Heritage Fellowship from the National Endowment for the Arts, the highest honor the nation bestows on its folk and traditional artists.[3] That was also the year the first-ever Cowboy Poetry Gathering was held in Elko, Nevada, sparking a national renaissance in cowboy poetry and music. Needless to say, Glenn was invited to perform and he became a mainstay of the event. He was invited back to perform at almost every subsequent Elko gathering (now the National Cowboy Poetry Gathering), where he was revered as the elder statesman of cowboy music.

Glenn was a multifaceted talent. In addition to being a singer, musician, and artist, he was also a leatherworker and saddlemaker, and he built his own stone house on his Arkansas Rafter O Ranch.

Glenn passed away February 11, 2015, shortly after returning home from what turned out to be his final performance, at the 32nd National Cowboy Poetry Gathering.

KEN OVERCAST

Born into a ranching family, Ken Overcast was reared in northern Montana on a section of the Milk River known as Paradise Valley. He grew up riding horses and attended a rural school with only three classmates. He and his wife, Dawn, who were childhood sweethearts, run a commercial cow-calf operation on Lodge Creek and also entertain audiences all over the West. Their ranch is located within fifteen miles of where both of their families have made their homes for more than one hundred years.[1] Dawn's family arrived around 1900, and Ken is related to the third white man to settle in that part of Montana.[2]

Ken first performed at a talent show at a Farmer's Union summer camp when he was nine years old. He sang Hank Williams's "I Heard That Lonesome Whistle Blow" a cappella. He had learned it from an old 78 rpm record his folks had that he'd nearly worn out. Ken recalls, "All the nine-year-old girls swooned, and I was hooked. I thought, 'Just think how much more they'll like me if I play a guitar, too.' So I started guitar lessons with a brand new Les Paul Special that my folks bought me."[3] Ken first played "professionally" in a high school trio in the 1960s; he played in several dance bands continuously until the early 1990s, when he started traveling solo. Ken says, "Ranching on a shoestring made weekend dance band income very attractive. It was something I could do after dark to help buy groceries and still keep the ranch going. We very rarely played over a hundred miles away from home, so we made it home the same night almost all the time. We went flat broke in the 1980s and lost absolutely everything. One of the only sources of income during that time was the gigs I got playing with the 'Busted Flat Band.'"[4]

DISCOGRAPHY

Silver and Gold, 1993
Thinkin' Back, 1994
Live!, 1995
Ken and Kalie Overcast (with daughter), 1997
Prairie Poetry, 1998
Montana Cowboy, 2000
Montana Campfire, 2001
Montana in My Soul, 2006

BOOKS

Yesterday's Yarns: Real Tales from the Real West, 2003
Shootin' the Breeze Cowboy Style, 2005
Tradin' Tales from a Montana Back Porch, 2007
Sittin' 'round the Stove: Stories from the Real West, 2008
Fables from the Far, Far West, 2011
The Way of the West from the Eye of a Cowboy, 2013

When Ken started writing songs, the first ten or fifteen he penned and recorded were gospel songs. In 1993 he established a music publishing company, Bear Valley Music, and the following year he founded Bear Valley Records and started working with Nashville producer Russ Ragsdale. Ken is also an author: He wrote a humor column called "Meadow Muffins" as well as a successful series of books of western short stories beginning in 2003. For a number of years, he also hosted *The Cowboy Show with Ken Overcast*, which featured both contemporary cowboy music and interviews and was syndicated on sixty-five radio stations coast to coast. In 2007 he and fellow Montanan Wylie Gustafson cowrote "Montana Lullaby," which was adopted by the state legislature as the state's official lullaby. Today Ken says, "We're not traveling near as much as we did in years past. Instead of running all over the place telling everyone how great it is to be a cowboy, I thought maybe I should just stay home and be one."[5]

AWARDS

Western Music Association, Yodeler of the Year, 1997

Academy of Western Artists, Will Rogers Award for Western Music Yodeler, 2000

True West magazine, Cowboy CD of the Year, *Montana Cowboy*, 2000

Will Rogers Medallion Award for Excellence in Western Fiction, *Sittin' 'round the Stove: Stories from the Real West*, 2009

HOWARD PARKER

DISCOGRAPHY

The Modern Day Cowboy (cassette)
Live and in Color (cassette)
Half and Half (cassette)

BOOKS

*Poetry and Prose from Horsethief
    Crossing*, 1977

Howard Parker was born in Gordon, Nebraska, in 1935. He was a fourth-generation Sandhills cowboy and rancher; a rodeo cowboy, announcer, and judge; and an avid Old West history buff and collector of western memorabilia. He was well known as a poet, singer, and musician and was featured at many cowboy poetry and music events, including the National Cowboy Poetry Gathering in Elko, Nevada; he even appeared on ABC's *Good Morning America*. Howard grew up on the family-owned Cross L Cattle Company Ranch south of Gordon, along the Niobrara River. He began his riding career at age two when his dad set him astride a spotted pony that his grandfather had won in a raffle. After graduating from high school, Howard cowboyed on the famous Spade Ranch near Ellsworth and then spent the next twenty years working for various cow outfits, playing in country bands, and rodeoing. Howard served as president of the Nebraska State Rodeo Association and competed in a variety of events. He was one of the top saddle bronc riders of the 1960s, winning the state championship in 1960, 1962, and 1963.[1] Howard died with his boots on, from a heart attack, while checking windmills on the family ranch in July 2004.

Howard Parker at Merriman, Nebraska, 1958

J PARSON

Cattleman, horseman, and musician J Parson grew up in Bakersfield, California, listening to the music of Buck Owens and Merle Haggard. J says,

> Buck Owens and Merle Haggard hit it big in the sixties when I was just a kid and at the time I never thought about how important that really was. But even now, wherever I perform, when people hear that I'm from Bakersfield, folks of all ages always say how much they like those guys and the Bakersfield sound. Buck and Merle aren't exactly what you would think of as cowboy singers but the stories they tell in their songs and the passion that can be heard have a great similarity to what is important in a good cowboy song. . . .
>
> I like to say I don't just sing cowboy songs but I sing songs cowboys like to listen to. Most of what I write is about real life situations that are part of the current time in which we live because that's what I know. To qualify as a cowboy song doesn't mean that the topic of the song has to be about something that happened a hundred years ago. Those old songs were written about current events that happened at that time. I love those old songs, and I sing them all the time, but there are a ton of folks out there that are living the cowboy life right now. They have important things that are happening to them right now. It's only natural that their stories be recorded in song.[1]

J has worked in the ranching business for most of his life. At various times he has run cattle from the Carrizo Plains to the Mojave Desert in

DISCOGRAPHY

J Parson Originals, 2003
Cowboy Nothin' More, 2005
Cowboy Tradition, 2006
I Ain't Leavin' without My Horse, 2007
The Eyes of a Cowboy, 2010
The Outlaw Trail, 2012

California. He also raises quality ranch horses and has been involved in the farming business in the San Joaquin Valley. J now splits his time between his ranch in California and his farm in southeast Kansas.

For many years J occasionally played at small gatherings, at family functions, after brandings, or with a few friends. Eventually, his family and friends convinced him that he should start playing in public. He has performed throughout the West, in California, Washington, Wyoming, Nevada, New Mexico, Kansas, Texas, and even as far east as Tennessee. He was a featured performer at the 2007 National Cowboy Poetry Gathering in Elko, Nevada. For more than two years, J provided the music for the RFD-TV network cooking show *Cowboy Flavor*.[2]

BOB PETERMANN

Bob Petermann was born and reared on a cow ranch in the remote Cedar Creek area of southwest Wibaux County, Montana. He and his wife, Kay, still live and work on the old family ranch. The Petermann ranch didn't receive electricity until 1966 or phone service until 1973, so the family was left to entertain itself. Bob's father played fiddle, his brother played guitar, and his sisters played the piano. Bob started playing at age eight when his brother taught him some guitar chords.[1] Today he has a repertoire of more than two hundred traditional and original songs. Bob draws on his life and ranching experience for the inspiration and content of his songs. His style of cowboy music has been described as "purist," which he considers a huge compliment. Bob has performed at cowboy poetry and music gatherings, county fairs, banquets, and other events around the West, including Old West Days in Valentine, Nebraska; Badger Clark Days in Hot Springs, South Dakota; and the Montana Cowboy Poetry Gathering in Lewistown. He also has been an invited performer at the National Cowboy Poetry Gathering in Elko, Nevada. He says, "What I love about performing is that I get to travel all around the country and meet the most wonderful people in the world. These are real people who work hard and do the right things, and I'm so blessed to get to sing for them."[2]

JEAN AND GARY PRESCOTT

Singer-songwriter Jean Prescott, known as "the Songbird of the Prairie," was born in Amarillo, Texas, and grew up on a ranch in West Texas. As a youngster she spent her summers horseback, helping out neighbors, and her evenings on the porch, playing her guitar and listening to her dad tell stories of his childhood on the big ranches in the panhandle of Texas. For the past twenty years, she has lived a bit south of Abilene with her husband, Gary, himself an accomplished singer and songwriter; they raise cattle and quarter horses. Gary and Jean met at the Texas Cowboy Poetry Gathering in Alpine in 1993. They married in 1994 and now frequently perform together, entertaining folks from the concert stage, around campfires, in churches, and in intimate living room concerts all across the country. Jean and Gary have both received numerous awards. Jean's repertoire includes cowboy and western, gospel, and western swing. She has crafted songs with several cowboy poets and songwriters, including Yvonne Hollenbeck, Gary McMahan, Debra Coppinger Hill, Doris Daley, Leon Autrey, Pat Richardson, and Joyce Woodson. Jean has released a number of CDs, including one with her husband and two as part of the group Sweethearts in Carharrts.

Jean hopes that her music "will bring to mind [people's] own family traditions and give a greater desire to preserve and pass them down to future generations."[1]

AWARDS

Academy of Western Artists, Western Music Female Vocalist of the Year, 1996 and 1997

Academy of Western Artists, Western Music Album of the Year, *Prairie Flowers*, 1998

Academy of Western Artists, Western Music Album of the Year, *An Inspirational Tapestry of the West*, 2002

Western Music Association, Best Collaboration Poet and Musician, "How Far is Lonesome," with Yvonne Hollenbeck, 2006

National Cowboy Symposium and Celebration, Award for Western Music, 2006

Western Music Association, Best Collaboration Poet and Musician, "Dining Out," with Yvonne Hollenbeck, 2008

BUCK RAMSEY

Kenneth Melvin Ramsey was born in New Home, Texas, on January 9, 1938. His father nicknamed him "Buckskin Tarbox," and the name Buck stuck with him for life. Buck was reared in a family of seven children—five girls and two boys. The children were raised in the Primitive Baptist Church, where they learned shape-note singing and harmony. The entire family was musical, and they frequently sang together at family gatherings. Four of Buck's sisters formed a gospel quartet and performed all over the Texas Panhandle. Buck was born with perfect pitch and sang in school choirs. By the time he was in high school, Buck was singing with a local band called the Sandy Swingsters, performing pop and jazz standards.[1]

Buck received his early education in a two-room schoolhouse in Middlewell, Texas, and graduated from Amarillo High School in 1956. He started college at Texas Tech but left to hitchhike around the country for a couple of years; he eventually returned to college at West Texas State. While in college he started working as a cowboy on ranches along the Canadian River in the Texas Panhandle, and he continued to cowboy until he was paralyzed in a horse accident in 1962 at age twenty-five. Buck said, "A sorry, spoiled horse named Cinnamon came undone" on him and some "bad ranch tack got tore up." Buck suffered a broken back and damaged spinal cord that put him in a wheelchair for the remainder of his life. Buck said about his cowboying days, "For some years back there I rode among the princes of the earth, full of health and hell and thinking punching cows was the one big show in the world. A horse tougher than me ended all that, and I have since been a stove-up cowpuncher trying to figure out how to write about the cowboy life."

DISCOGRAPHY
Rolling Uphill from Texas, 1992
My Home It Was in Texas, 1994
Buck Ramsey: Hittin' the Trail, 2003

BOOKS
And as I Rode Out on the Morning, 1993
A Christmas Waltz, 1996

AWARDS
National Cowboy Hall of Fame and Western Heritage Center, Wrangler Award for Outstanding Traditional Western Album, *Rolling Uphill from Texas* (1993) and *My Home It Was in Texas* (1995)
National Endowment for the Arts, National Heritage Fellowship, 1995

Buck Ramsey with Rooster Morris,
Texas Panhandle concert 1993

Buck taught himself to play the guitar after his accident. He grew up around cowboys and had heard cowboy songs his entire life. A particular influence was Buck's uncle, Ed Williams, his mother's brother. Uncle Ed ran away from home in his early teens to work as a cowboy and had picked up a bunch of old cowboy songs. Buck said, "I knew a lot of the old songs—my Uncle Ed was a great old cowboy. He gave me a Jack Thorpe songbook, one of the first collections printed of the real old traditional songs." After the accident Buck became progressively more interested in telling the story of what he always called his "cowboy tribe." Although he had started writing verse as a child, it was after his accident that he began seriously collecting and singing cowboy songs and writing poems.

Buck first came to the National Cowboy Poetry Gathering in Elko, Nevada, in 1989 and became an instant favorite. Buck returned for every Elko gathering after that. The cowboy poetry and music "movement" was a great inspiration, and Buck dedicated the remainder of his life to writing and singing about the cowboy. In 1992 Buck's first album, *Rolling Uphill from Texas*, issued by Fiel Publications, became an instant classic. He was awarded the Wrangler Award for Outstanding Traditional Western Album from the National Cowboy Hall of Fame and Western Heritage Center. In 1993 his sixty-three-page epic poem *And as I Rode Out on the Morning* was published by Texas Tech University Press. It is considered by many to be one of the finest pieces of western literature ever written. The prologue to the poem, "Anthem," has become a classic recitation. Buck's second album, *My Home It Was in Texas*, was released on cassette in 1994 and earned him a second Wrangler Award.

In 1995 Buck received a prestigious National Heritage Fellowship from the National Endowment for the Arts. In 1996 he also received the Lifetime Achievement Award and Best Poetry Book Award from the Academy of Western Artists and the American Cowboy Culture Award for Western Music.

Buck was considered by many the spiritual leader of the cowboy poetry movement. The Academy of Western Artists presents an annual award, named for him, for Best Poetry Book. In announcing the naming of the award, the AWA said,

Every now and then, a unique and very special person comes along who touches all of us in a memorable and lasting way. Buck was one of those rare individuals. Beside the considerable body of poetry and songs he left us, his quiet courage, his gentle friendship, his joyful sense of humor and his constant encouragement, both by example and by eloquent expression, left an indelible impression on those who knew him or ever saw him perform. The Academy of Western Artists is proud to announce, that to honor Buck's memory and keep it vital, the Poetry Book Award will hereafter be called "The Buck Ramsey Award."

Buck Ramsey passed away on January 3, 1998, at his home in Amarillo, Texas, one week before his sixtieth birthday. He had been scheduled to deliver the keynote address at the National Cowboy Poetry Gathering in Elko. In 2003 the Western Folklife Center and Smithsonian Folkways Records collaborated to release *Buck Ramsey: Hittin' the Trail*, a compilation of recorded live performances.

LUKE REED

Born and reared in Oklahoma, Luke Reed is the son of a ranch hand who was a founding member of the Cowboy's Turtle Association, now known as the Professional Rodeo Cowboys Association. He grew up around Ringling, working with old-time cowboys, and worked cattle with American Cattle Services during his college years. Growing up in feedlot country, he rode a lot of pens and worked for Hollis Dickey, Ronnie Austin, and the Goodnight Cattle Company.

Luke is a former member of the International Rodeo Association. A 1974 knee injury in a bulldogging accident ended his rodeo career. He graduated from Oklahoma State University in 1977 with a degree in agriculture education, and for some years he served as a county agriculture agent and later owned his own agriculture business.

Luke started playing guitar when he was the in the seventh grade. He says, "One of my friends got me interested, showed me my first three chords. My dad got a guitar for me and also showed me some more. I was attracted to it and I seemed to have a knack for it." He started writing in junior high school. "Mrs. Dion McKenzie got me started as a creative writer. She was our English teacher in junior high. [My creative writing] translated to songwriting pretty quickly, I guess, because I had inherited my dad's wild imagination and penchant for telling stories."[1]

In 1989 Luke moved to Nashville to pursue a career as a songwriter and musician. When Luke's dad found out that his son had quit his county agriculture agent job to play music, he said, "Son, how'd you find a business harder to make a living at than agriculture?" Luke's original country songs were recorded by George Strait, Gary Allen, David Ball, and Gene Watson. Luke is very proud of the fact that Hank Thompson and Johnny Bush are among those who have recorded his songs. In

DISCOGRAPHY

What's a Cowboy to Do?, 1989
The Cowboy and the Cattleman, 1993
Corridos: Story Songs of the West, 2000
Tried and True: Observations from the Big Circle, 2016

AWARDS

Academy of Western Artists, Will Rogers Award for Excellence in the Field of Western Arts, 1996
Academy of Western Artists, Western Swing Song of the Year, "Two Many Irons in the Fire," with Billy Caswell, 1997

addition, Luke's songs have been covered by Michael Martin Murphey, Red Steagall, Don Edwards, and many others. In 2001 Luke recorded an album for the Blue Hat label that featured his original western songs with guest appearances by Waylon Jennings, Bonnie Bramlett, Bill Miller, and Riders in the Sky. The album, *Corridos*, was nominated for a Grammy in the Best Contemporary Folk category. In 2003 Luke and his wife moved to Santa Fe, New Mexico, where he teaches agriculture at the Santa Fe Indian School. He cofounded and developed the school's Learning Horse Program, which provides horsemanship programs for at-risk Native American youth. He is certified in equine-assisted psychotherapy as a horse professional.

Today Luke is touring mostly solo, but occasionally with his eight-piece western swing band, the Modern Swing Pioneers. He says the players "are like a group of superheroes that can be called together at a moment's notice if the need arises for an all-star western swing band."[2]

He and wife Carol have a small place south of Santa Fe that he calls "Ranchito Poquito," where they keep a few good horses, dogs, and small livestock.

RAY REED

DISCOGRAPHY

Ray Reed Sings Traditional Frontier and Cowboy Songs, 1977

Ray Reed was born in San Jon, New Mexico, near the Texas border, east of Tucumcari, in 1916, of Irish, German, and Choctaw ancestry. He grew up around cowboying and music and learned many of his cowboy songs from his father. He recalled, "I was about ten or twelve when we used to play ranch dances in about a twenty-mile radius from my home town. That's where I learned to sing and play."[1] In the early 1930s he traveled to California, where there was a burgeoning western movie and music scene in Hollywood. He had a screen test but didn't go into the movies because he didn't like the Hollywood stereotype of the cowboy. Instead, he formed a touring western swing band called the Encinitas Ranch Hands. During the 1940s he played guitar with Bob Crosby's Cross Boys. In the late 1940s he worked as the ranch manager for the Mescalero Apache Tribe at Mescalero, New Mexico. Ray said, "I broke horses on the reservation and played music at night in the Navajo Lodge. I'd have to ride horseback when the snow got so deep I couldn't use my pickup to get from cow camp into town."[2] It was during this time, in 1949, that he met folklorist J. D. Robb, who recorded him singing about a dozen cowboy songs, released by Folkways Records much later, in 1977, as *Ray Reed Sings Traditional Frontier and Cowboy Songs*.

In later years Ray performed at the National Cowboy Poetry Gathering in Elko, Nevada, and in 1989 at the first National Cowboy Symposium and Celebration in Lubbock, Texas. He was inspired to return to New Mexico, where he started the Lincoln County Cowboy Symposium at the Rural Events Center in Glencoe in 1990. It has since become one of the best-known western music events in the country, with an emphasis on western swing. In 1998 Ray was again invited to perform at the National Cowboy Poetry Gathering in Elko; he was traveling home alone when he collapsed and died while refueling his Winnebago in Datil, New Mexico.

BRIGID REEDY

DISCOGRAPHY

*Limited Edition Brigid Reedy
EP, 2014*

One of the brightest young talents on the cowboy music scene is Brigid Reedy, a musician who has grown up homeschooled on ranches in Colorado and Montana. The daughter of musician, poet, and photographer John Reedy, she has been steeped in western music since she was born. Brigid first entertained crowds at the National Cowboy Poetry Gathering in 2003, at age two, by yodeling in the Pioneer Saloon, in the headquarters of the Western Folklife Center in Elko, Nevada.[1]

She began playing the fiddle a few years later. Her musical repertoire runs the full gamut of western music, from the most traditional cowboy tunes to new songs by contemporary singer-songwriters. Brigid has been an invited performer at events and gatherings, including the National Cowboy Poetry Gathering, the Monterey Cowboy Poetry and Music Festival, and Songs of the Cowboys.[2]

Brigid lives with her family near Boulder, Montana. She says, "Dad has been a wonderful influence on me my whole life. He gave me my first fiddle when I was five for my birthday and I started learning. And yodeling, I've been doing that since I was two. He taught it to me. And reciting poetry, my dad's a poet, so I've been exposed to it forever."[3] She frequently performs with her father, John, and brother Johnny. Brigid's first CD, an EP recorded live in January 2014, is a collection of five songs, a mix of original compositions and traditional tunes that highlight Brigid's fiddle playing and bright, clear voice.

Left: Reedy family busking
Right: Brigid on Splash, Inset: Brigid and Johnny Reedy

DAVE SCHILDT

DISCOGRAPHY

Still Kickin, 1988
No Ties, 1989
Indian Cowboy Songs and Ballads, 1990
Redboy in Nashville, 1994
Old Twisted Pine, 1995
Wild Horses, 2005

BOOKS

Redboy: The Indian Bull Rider, 2007

Dave "Redboy" Schildt was born in Killeen, Texas. His folks are both mixed-blood American Indians and, like Dave, enrolled members of the Blackfeet Tribe at Browning, Montana. He is a poet, musician, horse trainer, and schoolteacher and has worked as a stuntman for the Screen Actors Guild. He was an announcer, a working producer, and a competitor as a bull rider and bareback bronc rider in rodeo for twenty-eight years. Dave also coached high school and college rodeo, taught rodeo schools, and judged various events. During those twenty-eight years he collected about fourteen arm casts, a broken jaw, nine broken ribs, and a few concussions. He had to quit after an injury in 1997 during a bronc ride in which he won the Birch Creek United Indian Rodeo Association bareback championship.

Dave came by his interest in music through his family. He says, "All my uncles and my dad were singers and strummers."[1] His mother used to sing to him and his siblings with a guitar when they were kids. He learned to play in 1964, backing up his grandfather, who was a fiddler. He started playing for others at rodeos after being influenced by Chris LeDoux and started writing songs in 1979. He has performed at the Cowboy Songs and Range Ballads program in Cody, Wyoming; has been an invited performer at the National Cowboy Poetry Gathering in Elko, Nevada; and in 2004 he performed at the Smithsonian's George Gustav Heye Center in New York City. He recorded his first album in 1988 and then spent some time in Nashville in the early 1990s, working on his songwriting and recording his third album. In 2007 Dave published a book of his rodeo stories and memories, *Redboy: The Indian Bull Rider*. Recently, Dave has been working with Dust and Wire Productions as a consultant on a documentary film, *Indian Rodeo: Original American Cowboys*.

TRINITY SEELY

Trinity Seely was born into a musically talented ranching family in the cow country of the Chilcotin region of British Columbia. The family owned a guest ranch about six hundred miles north of the Canadian border, near the small town of Kleena Kleene. Growing up, Trinity learned to work hard, from the kitchen to the corral, on the ranch. "We were very isolated. My family ran the dude ranch just with our family. So my sisters and I ran the dude string and we cooked and cleaned cabins and entertained guests at night. Long as I can remember that's how we spent our time was on the back of a horse. As we got older, my sister that's older and I took over the dude string. Before I went off to school we had thirty head in our dude string."[1] Trinity and her sisters also started colts and trained them for packing and guest riding.

Trinity started writing songs at age thirteen. Her well-received first album, self-titled, was released in 2011, and she has released two more since then. She has been a featured performer at a number of cowboy and western events, including the National Cowboy Poetry Gathering in Elko, Nevada; the Heber City Cowboy Poetry and Music Festival in Utah; the Arizona Cowboy Poetry Gathering in Prescott; and other related events. In 2014 Trinity traveled to Germany to perform there. Today she and her family live on the Rex Ranch, near Ashby, in the Sandhills of Nebraska, where she continues to write songs from the viewpoint of a ranch wife and the mother of four ranch-reared children.

DISCOGRAPHY

Trinity Seely, 2011
Old Poly Rope, 2013
Cowboy's Wages, 2015

AWARDS

Western Music Association, Song of the Year, "A Cowboy Hat," 2014

CLYDE SPROAT

Clyde Halema`uma`u "Kindy" Sproat, one of the most revered of Hawaii's traditional singers, was born November 21, 1930, in the North Kohala district on the Big Island of Hawaii. The island is the home of some of the oldest and largest cattle ranches in the country, such as the 133,000-acre Parker Ranch. Cattle were introduced to the islands in 1793 and in the 1830s.

King Kamehameha III brought over Mexican vaqueros to teach the Hawaiians how to work cattle. They also brought their guitars with them. The Hawaiian cowboys were called *paniolos*, derived from the Spanish word *Español*. Music has always been a large part of *paniolo* culture. Kindy's paternal great-grandfather, Jose Ramone Baesa, was one of the first vaqueros brought to the islands. Kindy's grandfather, J. W. Sproat, was a Missouri muleskinner who came to Hawaii in 1893 as part of the militia that overthrew the Hawaiian monarchy. He stayed on and married Kindy's Hawaiian grandmother, Clara Kalehua`opele.

Kindy grew up packing mules into Honokane Iki, an isolated valley two hours away from the end of the road, where his family lived. The only transportation to the valley was by mule pack train. Kindy's father was part Hawaiian and he worked on the Kohala Ditch Trail, maintaining the waterways that fed the great sugar plantations of the early and middle twentieth century.[1] Kindy worked for the Anna Ranch in Waimea when he was a teenager, and later he worked with his brother Buzzy, leading mule rides on the island of Molokai from 1974 to 1979. He was a guide and also sang as they rode the 1,700-foot trail down the highest sea cliffs in the world to Kalaupapa, in Kalaupapa National Historical Park.

Kindy remembered how, every night after the evening meal, his Hawaiian mother would play the banjo and sing to the children. Later, the family relocated to Niuli`i, which was closer to schools, churches, and restaurants on Hawaii island. Kindy liked to stop at local saloons and listen to the master slack key guitar players of the time. He said,

> That sound and rhythm has haunted me all my growing years, and even until this day I listen for the old sweet rhythm of the old slack key. Slack key has changed considerably since I was a boy. Like the old-time slack key, the old-time folk songs of Hawaii have faded into the past. I love the old songs, so I hang onto them and sing them just as I heard them sung. . . . I had a special feeling for the old Hawaiian songs. The tunes haunted me. I sang, whistled, and hummed them constantly.[2]

He particularly loved the songs of the *paniolos*. According to the National Endowment for the Arts, which awarded Kindy a National Heritage Fellowship in 1988, he "learned to play the four-stringed ukulele and liked the straightforward accompaniment of the slack key guitar for his Hawaiian songs. . . . Over the years, Sproat developed a repertoire of more than four hundred songs. He has preserved the music that originated for the most part in the early twentieth century and reflected the changes in Hawaiian musical traditions from ancient chanted forms accompanied by percussion instruments to falsetto singing and Western melodic forms accompanied by the ukulele and slack key guitar."[3] In later years he frequently played with *paniolo* slack key guitarist Karin Haleamau. Kindy performed at local events, luaus, family gatherings, nursing homes, and in concerts. He was invited to perform at the National Cowboy Poetry Gathering, in Elko, Nevada, and was part of the National Council for the Traditional Arts' Cowboy Tour in 1983. Kindy passed away in December 2008.

DAVE STAMEY

DISCOGRAPHY

Buckaroo Man, 1997
Tonopah, 1999
Campfire Waltz, 2000
Wheels, 2001
If I Had a Horse, 2003
Old Friends, 2007
Come Ride with Me, 2009
Twelve Mile Road, 2011
Live in Sana Ynez, 2014

AWARDS

Western Music Association,
    Male Performer of the Year,
    2000, 2006, 2007, 2008,
    2011, and 2012
Academy of Western Artists,
    Western Music Male Vocalist
    of the Year, 2001
Western Music Association,
    Songwriter of the Year,
    2005, 2007, 2010, and 2012
Western Music Association,
    Entertainer of the Year,
    2006, 2008, 2009, 2010,
    2012, 2013, 2014, and 2015

Dave and his wife, Melissa,
leading a pack trip in the
Cascade Valley, Sierra Nevada

Cowboys & Indians magazine has called Dave Stamey "the Charlie Russell of western music." He has been a cowboy, a mule packer, and a dude wrangler. Originally from Montana, where the family's home ranch was, Dave grew up in the ranching business. He was reared on the Central California coast, in the area south of Paso Robles around San Luis Obispo. Later he began packing mules for trail rides up around Bishop and Mammoth Lakes, which he did for some years, taking tourists into the Sierra backcountry with horses and mules.

Originally an aspiring novelist and prose writer, Dave learned to play guitar at age twelve and switched to songwriting in the mid-1990s. "I had no connection to mainstream country music," he recalled in a 2012 interview. "I'm a songwriter and I needed to write about what I know. Being a cowboy, I naturally drifted into what I knew."[1] His influences range from Marty Robbins and Ian Tyson to John Steinbeck. Dave has become one of the most respected and popular western entertainers, performing at venues around the country, and he has won numerous awards and accolades. *True West* magazine proclaimed him the Best Living Western Solo Musician in three different years, and *Western Horseman* magazine included his "Vaquero Song" in its list of the thirteen best cowboy songs of all time.

GAIL STEIGER

Gail Steiger describes himself as a "cowpuncher/ranch manager/ filmmaker/songwriter who is still trying to decide what he wants to be when he grows up."[1] Gail comes from a background of both ranching and songwriting. His great-grandfather came to Prescott, Arizona, in the 1870s, and he and his son had a ranch in Skull Valley. Gail and his twin brother, Lew, were born on the Bar Heart Ranch near Williams, Arizona. Their father was Sam Steiger, former Republican Arizona state senator and US congressman from Arizona from 1967 to 1977, and also an avid rancher. Growing up, Gail worked on and off on his father's ranches but says he never "had in mind to punch cows."[2] He graduated from Colorado College in Colorado Springs with a business degree. Still, he later drifted back into cowboying and became a full-time hand on the Cross U and Spider Ranches in Yavapai County, Arizona. He has been the foreman of the sprawling Spider Ranch, sixty-eight sections of some of the roughest ranching country in Arizona, since 1995; he now runs the property with his wife, Amy, an accomplished novelist. Gail was greatly influenced by his grandfather, Arizona cowboy and revered cowboy poet Gail Gardner, who wrote such classic cowboy songs as "Tying the Knots in the Devil's Tail" (aka "The Sierry Petes") and "The Dude Wrangler."

Gail is an accomplished songwriter and performer whose songs reflect contemporary ranching and cowboy life. He has been writing songs for more than thirty years. Sometimes the songs are about cowboys, and sometimes they're about a cowboy's take on life. In 2007 he released a CD, *The Romance of Western Life*, of which *American Cowboy* magazine said, "Cowboy folk is about the best way to describe this album . . . kinda like listening to Bob Dylan if Dylan had been a working cowboy. The best part is that the lyrics are so beautifully descriptive of daily

cowboy life." In 2015 Gail released *A Matter of Believin'*, a remarkable two-CD set that includes songs and stories of his family's ranching experience. He has performed at numerous cowboy music and poetry events around the West, including the Arizona Cowboy Poet's Gathering in Prescott, the Texas Cowboy Poetry Gathering in Alpine, and the National Cowboy Poetry Gathering in Elko, Nevada.

In 1987 Gail and his brother made a documentary film called *Ranch Album* that was released as a national PBS special. It is considered one of the best portrayals of modern cowboy and ranching life on film. In addition to running the Spider Ranch, Gail continues to operate Steiger Brothers Video with Lew, through which they work on various films and multimedia projects. With Lorraine Rawls, Gail filmed and produced the documentary *Gardian Nation*, about the French cowboys of the Camargue region of southern France. He has traveled to Mongolia, Brazil, Argentina, France, Spain, and Hungary with the Western Folklife Center in connection with its cultural exchange program, as both a videographer and a performer. He is working on a documentary project about cowboys around the world. The US State Department invited Gail to travel to Afghanistan and Turkmenistan to work with the US embassies in Kabul and Ashgabat to connect some American cowboys with Afghan and Turkmen horsemen and herders.

Left: Gail with T. R. Stewart at campsite in
Pasayten Wilderness, Washington, 2006

T. R. STEWART

Packer T. R. Stewart was born in Puyallup, Washington, and like most little kids grew up enamored of the cowboys he saw on television. He saw his first actual cowboys when he was about five, at the Puyallup Fairgrounds, and he was hooked. He started playing music when he was thirteen. His older sister was interested in folk music and got a Mexican guitar from Juarez. His sister didn't make much progress with the guitar, so T. R. got it and started learning to play it. He developed his singing with the Baptist Youth Chorus, where he was called on to do some solos. After high school T. R. enrolled in college in Ellensburg, Washington, as an art major. While he was in college, he lived with a friend who had quarter horses, which finally gave T. R. the opportunity to work with horses. As an art major he was drawn to the trappings of the West: saddles, bits, and other artistic expressions of horse culture. It was during this time that T. R. started writing his own songs.

After graduating from college, T. R. didn't find an art gig, so he headed out to pursue other opportunities. He got a job wrangling horses for the Hidden Valley Ranch near Boulder, Colorado, and he also sang and played for ranch guests. Eventually, T. R. drifted back to Puyallup and got a job caring for the horses at the Puyallup Fairgrounds and creating the artwork for the fairground's signs, which he did for fifteen years. During this time he also ventured over to Tacoma to perform at Victory Music's open mic nights, got more serious about his music, and started playing small gigs and for western and cowboy events. T. R. then met Methow Valley packer John Doran through Back Country Horsemen and started working with him, setting up hunting camps, wrangling horses, and packing mules. T. R. liked the physicality of the work. When Doran sold his back country permit to Cascade Wilderness Outfitters,

DISCOGRAPHY
Long Shadows, 2002

a third-generation family outfit, T. R. went to work for them and has now been packing in the Paysaten Wilderness and Lake Chelan-Sawtooth Wilderness for twenty years. T. R. has always enjoyed sharing his songs at the campfire on the pack trips. In 2002 he recorded a CD, *Long Shadows*. He has performed at cowboy events such as the Ellensburg Spirit of the West Cowboy Gathering and the National Cowboy Poetry Gathering.

LINDA SVENDSEN

Few packers have had experience as varied as Linda Svendsen, who has led pack trips in half a dozen countries on three continents. Growing up in Oregon, she was riding by the time she was six, and by age ten she had ridden in every national park in the West and was "working" as an assistant to local wranglers and guides. She started singing early as well. Linda recalls, "My dad was always singing, and I started singing with him when he'd take me on road trips to his favorite fishing holes. 'Home on the Range' is the first song I can remember hearing him sing, and I learned it from him. I was probably eight years old."[1] She got a ukulele when she was ten and graduated to a Sears mail-order Silvertone acoustic guitar when she was twelve, which her brother taught her to play. She had her first "band" when she was in the eighth grade, called the Halos, and they sang folk songs like "Blowin' in the Wind" and "500 Miles."

Linda got involved in adventure travel while she was a student at Prescott College in Arizona and began leading hiking and mountaineering trips for the college in the early 1970s. Later that decade she and her future husband, Kent Madin, led canoeing trips in the Yukon and hiking trips in Bolivia. They then moved on to Baja California, where they conducted sea kayaking, whale watching, and mountain biking trips, as well as rides on mules into the remote cave paintings in central Baja. In 1985 they started Boojum Expeditions, an adventure travel company ("Uncommon Travel") based in Bozeman, Montana. That same year Linda researched, designed, and led the first-ever commercial horseback trip in central Asia in Inner Mongolia, China. She continued to lead trips in Inner Mongolia for several years. In 1986 Linda ran the first horse trip in eastern Tibet; she continued those trips almost annually until 2005. In 1988 she led the first pack trip in the Altai Mountains in

Packing into the Bob Marshall Wilderness Area, Montana

northwest China, and she did those for several years thereafter. In the mid-1990s Linda started leading rides in Patagonia (southern Argentina) in the Nahuel Huapi Park area near Bariloche. Also during the 1990s she co-led pack trips in Yellowstone National Park with a local outfitter. Boojum Expeditions began horse programs in Outer Mongolia in 1993, and Linda led many trips there, in central and northern Mongolia. Beginning in 2005 she led horse trips for three years in northern Kyrgyzstan. With the exception of the weeklong rides in Yellowstone, all of the trips were three to four weeks in length, and except for Argentina, all the trips were pack trips using local horses, yaks, or camels for pack stock. Riders rode local stock, on local saddles, and rode with the local nomads or gauchos hired as wranglers.[2]

All during this time Linda continued to pursue music, performing with the Thistle Sisters, who did cowboy songs as well as old-time music and gospel; with the bluegrass group the Pine Creek Ramblers; and with the cowboy band New Frontier. In 2005 the US State Department sent Linda, along with Hal Cannon and Ron Kane, to Kyrgyzstan to represent American cowboy music as part of its cultural exchange programs; in 2011 she traveled to Afghanistan with Gail Steiger; and in 2013 she went to Turkmenistan with Hal Cannon, Gail Steiger, and Andy Hedges. Linda and Boojum Expeditions also facilitated "cowboy to cowboy" exchange programs to Mongolia, Brazil, Argentina, France, and Spain for the Western Folklife Center and the National Cowboy Poetry Gathering.

Linda still lives in Bozeman with her horses, husband, and cats. She and Kent are in the process of turning Boojum over to their Mongolian staff, thereby making Boojum Expeditions a solely Mongolian owned and operated company. She sings with a couple of different local bands and spends her time horseback in the mountain ranges of southwest Montana.

CAITLYN TAUSSIG

Caitlyn Leigh Taussig was born in Kremmling, Colorado, in, 1986, the fourth generation of Taussigs in Grand County. The Taussig family had a hotel in downtown Denver but came up north and bought property on Ute Pass in the late 1800s. They bought a ranch that is now under the tailings pond for a molybdenum mill. They raised and showed Herefords all over the country, and her dad would ride the train cars with the cattle. They had a couple of different ranches down the Williamsfork Valley, and Caitlyn grew up on one of them. When she was fourteen her dad and his brother sold that ranch and split up. Her part of the family ended up on a ranch north of Kremmling, where she now runs cow-calf

pairs with her mother and sister. Caitlyn started riding when she was five, already helping with the ranch work, and has been at it ever since. Today she trains horses in the Californio tradition and is the county 4-H coordinator.

Caitlyn got her first guitar when she was eight. She says, "I took lessons from a couple local people, and I think I wrote my first song when I was nine or ten. It was a ballad about the prince and the pauper! I think I realized I could sing when I was in the sixth grade, but my guitar teacher told my folks I could sing when I was eight. I used to sing old cowboy songs. My dad always sang, and we used to duet on the national anthem."[1]

Caitlyn grew up listening to Joan Baez, Bob Dylan, and Ian Tyson with her mom, and Marty Robbins and Chris LeDoux with her dad. Today she's influenced by "everyone—all of my friends who play cowboy music as well as Steve Earle, Guy Clark, Corb Lund, and the like."[2] Caitlyn's first "public" performance was opening for Baxter Black in her hometown in the sixth grade. She played bluegrass in high school and sang the national anthem for sports events and rodeos. She started playing cowboy music in public at the first Annual Early Californio Skills of the Rancho roping event in Santa Ynez, California, in 2013. She has played numerous events and venues since, including the Grand Encampment Cowboy Gathering, the Badger Clark Cowboy Poetry Gathering, the Grand Junction Cowboy Poetry Gathering, the Durango Cowboy Poetry Gathering, and the National Cowboy Poetry Gathering in Elko, Nevada.

ROD TAYLOR

DISCOGRAPHY

Ridin' Down the Canyon, 1990
A Philmont Collection, 1995
Here, There, Anywhere, 2010
The Rifters (the Rifters), 2004
The Great River (the
   Rifters), 2011
Live at the Sagebrush (the
   Rifters), 2013

Cowboy, singer, and songwriter Rod Taylor currently cowboys on the Philmont Ranch, near Cimarron, New Mexico, which is owned and operated by the Boy Scouts of America. Although the emphasis is on scouting, Philmont remains a working cattle ranch. Philmont has about 300 horses, 250 cows, 100 burros, and 100 buffalo on 137,000 acres. Rod is responsible for the cowherd and lends a hand with the additional livestock.[1] Originally from Lubbock, Texas, Rod started his cowboy career while in high school and college at both the C Bar and Philmont Ranches. After taking a stab at college, he left home to pursue the cowboy life. He worked at the Vermejo Park, TO, UU, and Little Horn Ranches before ending up back at the Philmont Ranch in 1983, where he has been ever since.

Rod started singing early in church and school choirs, and both of his parents were music lovers. He got his first guitar when he was in the sixth grade, and in high school he and some friends formed a band. "We played bluegrass music," he says. "We played rock and roll. We played country music. We played folk music."[2] Rod counts as influences everyone from Roy Acuff, Hank Williams, and Bob Wills to Bob Dylan, the Beatles, and fellow Lubbock musicians Jimmie Dale Gilmore, Butch Hancock, and Joe Ely. After moving to New Mexico, his musical activity was mostly sitting in for a few numbers on weekends with bands in Taos and Red River. Then, in the late 1980s, he decided to get more serious, and he started playing some solo gigs at various cowboy poetry and music events and sites, including the National Cowboy Symposium in Lubbock, Texas; the National Cowboy and Western Heritage Museum in Oklahoma City; the Nara Visa Cowboy Gathering in New Mexico; and the National Cowboy Poetry Gathering in Elko, Nevada. In 1990 he recorded

Rod Taylor performing with his band, The Rifters

and released *Ridin' Down the Canyon*. Not long after, he and some friends formed a band called the Rounders that appeared in the Martin Scorsese film *The Hi-Lo Country*. In 2002 Rod's present band, the Rifters, was formed, playing what they call "acoustic southwestern Americana" music. Today Rod continues to live with his wife, Patty, at the Philmont Ranch and perform both solo and with the Rifters.

IAN TYSON

Singer, songwriter, and rancher Ian Dawson Tyson was born to British immigrants in Victoria, British Columbia, in 1933, and grew up in Duncan, British Columbia. When he was nineteen Ian "caught the rodeo fever" and started riding bareback broncs. In 1956 a bronc threw him and stepped on his ankle and shattered it. He spent some time in the hospital recovering from the accident. To while away the time he borrowed a guitar from another patient in the room and started trying to learn to play. Ian made his singing debut at the Heidelberg Café in Vancouver, Britsh Columbia, in 1956 and played with a rock 'n' roll band, the Sensational Stripes.[1]

Ian graduated from the Vancouver School of Art in 1958 and worked for a while as a commercial artist in Toronto. Coincidentally, he arrived just in time for the folk boom of the late 1950s and early 1960s. He met Sylvia Fricker, and they formed the popular folk duo Ian and Sylvia and toured North America, playing the music circuits. The two eventually married. In 1969 they formed and fronted the group the Great Speckled Bird, a proto-country-rock band. Beginning in 1970 the duo also began hosting a television show, *Nashville North*, which became *The Ian Tyson Show* when the couple split up in the middle of the decade.[2] Ian gave the Nashville, Tennessee, music scene a try but was disillusioned and moved back to Alberta. He took a job as a ranch hand at the Pincher Creek Ranch for a couple of years, occasionally playing for rodeos.[3] In 1978 Neil Young recorded a cover of the Ian and Sylvia folk hit "Four Strong Winds," and Ian was able to buy the T-Bar-Y Ranch near Longview, Alberta. He devoted most of his time to working with cutting horses and cattle. In 1985 Ian was

DISCOGRAPHY

Ol' Eon, 1973
One Jump Ahead of the Devil, 1978
Old Corrals and Sagebrush, 1983
Ian Tyson, 1984
Cowboyography, 1987
I Outgrew the Wagon, 1989
And Stood There Amazed, 1991
Eighteen Inches of Rain, 1994
All the Good 'Uns, 1996
Lost Herd, 1999
Live at Longview, 2002
Songs from the Gravel Road, 2005
Yellowhead to Yellowstone and Other Love Stories, 2008
Songs from the Stone House, 2011
Raven Singer, 2012
All the Good 'Uns Vol. 2, 2013
Carnero Vaquero, 2015

invited to Elko for Nevada's first Cowboy Poetry Gathering. There he met some of the authentic cowboys who were singing and reciting cowboy poetry, and he felt encouraged to increase his focus on writing songs about cowboy life and the contemporary West.

In the ensuing years Ian has continued to cement his position as the West's preeminent songwriter, penning many songs that have become classics. In 2006 he sustained irreversible scarring to his vocal cords as a result of a concert at the Havelock Country Jamboree followed a year later by a virus contracted during an airplane flight. This resulted in a notable loss of the remarkable quality and range for which he was known. He described his new sound as "gravelly." Fortunately, with the help of doctors and voice coaches, he was able to regain his voice. Now in his eighties, he continues to perform, write, and record but says he had to "quit the horses" after a young horse bucked him off and almost put him in the hospital. In 2010 Ian published a memoir, *The Long Trail: My Life in the West*, cowritten with Calgary journalist Jeremy Klaszus. Ian has also written a book of young adult fiction about his song "La Primera," called *La Primera: The Story of Wild Mustangs*.[4]

AWARDS

Alberta Recording Industry Association
Male Performer of the Year, 1987
Country Artist of the Year, 1987
Song of the Year, "Navajo Rug," 1987
Album of the Year, *Cowboyography*, 1987
Single of the Year, "Fifty Years Ago," 1988
Best Country Artist on Record, 1988
Male Recording Artist of the Year, 1988
Composer of the Year, 1989
Performer of the Year, 1989

Big Country Awards (Canada)
Outstanding Male Performance, 1975
Best Country Album, *Ol' Eon, 1975*
Top Country TV Show, *The Ian Tyson Show*, 1975
Artist of the Year, 1988
Top Male Vocalist, 1988
Best Album, *Cowboyography*, 1988

Canadian Country Music Association
Male Vocalist of the Year, 1987 and 1988
Single of the Year, "Navajo Rug," 1987
Album of the Year, *Cowboyography*, 1987
Inducted into Canadian Country Music Hall of Fame, 1989
Video of the Year, "Springtime in Alberta," 1991

Country Music Association of Calgary
Top Alberta Male Vocalist of the Year, 1989
Top Alberta Song of the Year, "Fifty Years Ago," 1989
Top Alberta Single of the Year, "Fifty Years Ago," 1989
Favorite Calgary and Area Country Entertainer, 1989

Juno Awards (Canada)
Country Music Vocalist of the Year, 1987
Inducted into Juno Hall of Fame (with Sylvia Tyson), 1992

Songs from the Gravel Road TV Documentary
Bronze Medal, 54th New York Festivals International Television and Film
    Awards, 2011
Gold Remi Award, Best TV Documentary, 44th Houston Independent Film
    Festival, 2011

Other
ASCAP Country Award, "Someday Soon," 1992
Prairie Music Awards, Outstanding Country Recording, "Lost Herd," 1999
American Cowboy Culture Awards, Western Music Award, 2000
Inducted into Prairie Music Hall of Fame, 2001
National Cowboy and Western Heritage Museum, Wrangler Award for
    Outstanding Original Western Composition, "Bob Fudge," 2002
Inducted into British Columbia Country Music Association Hall of
    Fame, 2006
Inducted into Western Music Hall of Fame, 2008
Western Horseman magazine's Horseman of the Year Award, 2009
Canadian Museum of Civilization, Resonance Award for a Lifetime
    Contribution to Canadian Music, 2009

JESSIE VEEDER

Singer-songwriter Jessie Veeder grew up on a three-thousand-acre fourth-generation family ranch at the edge of the Badlands of western North Dakota. Jessie says, "This is where my great-grandfather came to create a living and raise a family, and it is where I grew up singing and writing music and riding horses and learning to appreciate nature and family and space."[1] The Veeder Ranch is isolated, as is the town in which Jessie grew up—but it sits on top of one of the country's largest oil reserves, and western North Dakota has found itself in the middle of one of the biggest economic booms the country has seen.[2] Jessie sings about ranching life but also about her experience of the huge oil boom.

Jessie's father, himself a musician, has influenced her songwriting, and they frequently perform together onstage. He was always interested in songwriting and encouraged her to try the craft when she was twelve or thirteen. Jessie released her first album when she was just sixteen. After the release of her third album, *Jessie Veeder Live*, which she recorded with her father's hometown band, Lonesome Willy, Jessie moved back home to her family's ranch; she had been away for ten years. Jessie has been a featured artist at the National Cowboy Poetry Gathering in Elko, Nevada, and a main stage act at the Red Ants Pants Music Festival in White Sulphur Springs, Montana.

Jessie has a degree in communications and public relations from the University of North Dakota, has been a professional fundraiser for the University of Montana–Missoula and Dickinson State University, and owns a small communications business.[3] Her popular website "Meanwhile, Back at the Ranch . . ." chronicles life on the Veeder Ranch. The success of this website landed her a job as a weekly columnist for Forum Communications and newspapers across the state, and as a commentator on Prairie Public Radio.

JOHNNY WHELAN

DISCOGRAPHY

The Cowboy Tour: A National Tour of Cowboy Songs, Poetry, Big Windy Stories, Humor, and Fiddling (compilation), 2000

Johnny Whelan carries the name of his Irish great-grandfather, who went to Mexico in revolutionary times, but he is of predominantly Mexican and Yaqui Indian ancestry. He grew up as a working vaquero on the Sierra Bonita Ranch, near Willcox, Arizona. He began riding at age eight and began entering rodeos as a teenager. He says he learned the vaquero trade the traditional way, "by getting skinned up a lot."

His father started him on the fiddle when he was nine, but he eventually chose the guitar as his instrument. Reared on the border, Johnny grew up singing *corridos*, the narrative songs that celebrate the lives, times, and loves of bandits, smugglers, heroes, and historical events. Johnny plays guitar and uses a rack-mounted Echo Harp, a tremolo harmonica with the top and bottom holes purposely tuned slightly off from each other, to produce a vibrato effect. He uses this to great effect to simulate the parts usually played by the accordion in *Norteño* music. The family has a shared interest in the songs and dances that were taught to Johnny by his parents and grandparents, and Johnny and his wife have passed them on to their children and grandchildren. They often perform together as the Whelan Family. In 1983 Johnny was part of the Cowboy Tour orchestrated by the National Council for the Traditional Arts, along with Glenn Ohrlin, Brownie Ford, and Clyde Sproat, also included in this book. Two of his live performances from the tour are included on a compilation CD produced by the council.

HUB WHITT

Hub Whitt was born near Thermopolis, Wyoming, the oldest of six kids born to a ranching family. Hub and his identical twin brother, Hugh, were raised horseback and were riding before they could walk. Hub learned to work livestock from his folks and the neighboring ranchers. The family moved around to ranches throughout the region when he was young. At different times they lived in a sheep wagon, an old stage station that sat on the original route from Casper to Yellowstone National Park, a homemade lean-to that his father built onto an existing cabin, and a log cabin in Canada for a winter. At the age of eleven, Hub was working on a neighbor's ranch for the summer, and he had a job every summer after that, working for different ranches in the area. When they were fourteen Hub and his brother went out on the spring roundup for the big Grieves Ranch. Looking back, Hub says that was as close as he ever got to working like they did in the "old days."

Hub suffered a gunshot wound in his right leg when he was eighteen, and his leg had to be amputated above the knee. He tried college for a year after that but went back to ranch work. Hub continued to work on ranches and drifted to Arizona in the fall of 1979, where he spent almost a year working on a ranch near Globe. "I thought I was a pretty good cowboy until I got to Arizona. I had never been in the brush, and I learned real quick that just because you saw them didn't mean you had them."[1] Hub drifted up to Montana, worked on some ranches there, and eventually wound up in Cody, Wyoming, and started guiding big game hunters every fall. "I guided every fall for fifteen years straight, and some of the years, I hired on working the spring bear hunts, would pack people in to fishing camps all summer, and then guide all fall."[2]

Hub got started in music at an early age:

I can remember the neighbors coming over, and some of them would bring along a guitar, and would sit and sing. I grew up listening to everything from "Little Joe the Wrangler" to "Crazy Arms." I liked it all, and I can still remember my dad singing "Tying the Knots in the Devil's Tail" when I was two or three years old. I grew up around all those old cowboy songs, and I thought everybody knew them. It was only after I started going to Cowboy Songs and Range Ballads in Cody, Wyoming, that I found out it was considered "art" or "folk music," and people were willing to pay good money to listen to me sing them. I was tickled to death.[3]

Hub traveled from 1990 through 1993, playing music full time. During the summer of 1992, he opened for Chris LeDoux in Montana, Wyoming, and Idaho, and during the next few years, Hub appeared on stage with such acts as Baxter Black, Riders of the Purple Sage, Jean Prescott, and Brenn Hill. An accomplished songwriter, Hub has won awards from *American Songwriter* magazine for his compositions "One More Rodeo" and "When the Nighthawk Hollered Horses." His music has been recorded by artists in Montana, Wyoming, and Nebraska. Today he is writing songs and poetry and performing throughout the year. Hub has released two CDs, and his son Tucker is now following in Hub's footsteps. He still rides and works cattle, and he and Tucker are playing music together. Hub got bucked off and cracked some ribs in the spring of 2015, after which he said, "I have never been hurt bad in a horse wreck 'til now, and that includes the three times I've been hung up and drug! I got back on and finished that day's ride, and I kept riding every day that spring, but I took it pretty easy. I'm sixty years old, and the ground just isn't soft anymore."[4]

ENDNOTES

Jesse Ballantyne

1. Jesse Ballantyne, *Cowboy Serenade* album notes, CD Baby Music Store, www.cdbaby.com/cd/ballantyne (accessed August 30, 2015).
2. Cathy Orr, "High Definition," *American Cowboy*, November–December 2003.

Mike Beck

1. "Horses," Mike Beck Music and Horses, http://mikebeck.com/horses (accessed September 3, 2015).
2. As quoted in "Mike Beck," CowboyPoetry.com, www.cowboypoetry.com/mikebeck.htm (accessed September 3, 2015).
3. Ibid.

Adrian Brannan

1. "Adrian," Adrian Brannan website, www.buckaroogirl.com/biography (accessed March 7, 2016).

Dale Burson and Family

1. *Texas Highways*, "Don't Fence Me In: Cowboy Crooners through the Years," July 13, 2012, www.texashighways.com/the-magazine/item/1667-don-t-fence-me-in-cowboy-crooners-through-the-years (accessed March 7, 2016).

Lyle Cunningham

1. Montana Obituary and Death Notice Archive, p. 732, www.genlookups.com/mt/webbbs_config.pl/noframes/read/372 (accessed September 3, 2015).
2. Ibid.

Stephanie Davis

1. Author interview with Stephanie Davis, July 21, 2015.
2. "Featured at the Bar-D Ranch: Stephanie Davis," CowboyPoetry.com, www.cowboypoetry.com/stephaniedavis.htm (accessed July 15, 2015).
3. "Stephanie Davis (singer)," Wikipedia, https://en.wikipedia.org/wiki/Stephanie_Davis_(singer) (accessed July 15, 2015).

Geno Delafose

1. Bill Nevins, "Geno Delafose," RootsWorld, www.rootsworld.com/rw/feature/delafose.html (accessed September 8, 2015).

Juni Fisher

1. "About Juni," Juni Fisher website, www.junifisher.net/juniFisherBio.html (accessed December 19, 2015).
2. Ibid.
3. "Featured at the Bar-D Ranch: Juni Fisher," CowboyPoetry.com, www.cowboypoetry.com/junifisher.htm (accessed December 19, 2015).

Brownie Ford

1. "Thomas Edison Ford," NEA National Heritage Fellowships, www.arts.gov/honors/heritage/fellows/thomas-edison-ford (accessed December 19, 2015).
2. Nicholas R. Spitzer, "Brownie Ford: Lifelines of a Woods Cowboy," Folklife in Louisiana, www.louisianafolklife.org/LT/Articles_Essays/brownie_ford.html (accessed December 20, 2015).
3. "Thomas Edison Ford," NEA National Heritage Fellowships.
4. Spitzer, "Brownie Ford."
5. Ibid.

Ryan Fritz

1. Author interview with Ryan Fritz, September 7, 2015.
2. Ibid.

D. W. Groethe

1. As quoted on "Featured at the Bar-D Ranch: DW Groethe," CowboyPoetry.com, www.cowboypoetry.com/dwgroethe.htm (accessed August 12, 2015).
2. Alexandra Swaney, "D. W. Groethe: MonDak Original," American Folklife Center of the Library of Congress, www.loc.gov/folklife/events/HomegrownArchives/0405-folklifeconcerts_files/Groethe.pdf (accessed August 12, 2015).

Wylie Gustafson

1. "Biography," Wylie Gustafson website, www.wyliewebsite.com/press/biopgrahy (accessed March 10, 2016).

2. Shelly Kurz, "Wylie Gustafson," *Western Horseman*, November 2001, reprinted at www.wyliewebsite.com/press/reviews/western-horseman-magazine-november-2001 (accessed March 10, 2016).
3. "Biography," Wylie Gustafson website.

Kenny Hall

1. "Kenny Hall," Cowboy Poets of Utah, www.cowboypoetsofutah.org/members.html (accessed August 25, 2015; biographical content since deleted).
2. Ibid.

Joni Harms

1. "Biography," Joni Harms website, www.joniharms.com/bio.html (accessed March 10, 2016).

Kristyn Harris

1. "Kristyn Harris," Lost n Lava Cowboy Gathering, www.lostnlavagathering.com/kristyn-harris.html (accessed August 23, 2015).
2. "About," Kristyn Harris website, http://kristynharris.com/bio (accessed August 23, 2015).

Don Hedgpeth

1. J. P. S. Brown, "In the Grand Tradition," *American Cowboy*, May-June 1975.
2. Author interview with Don Hedgpeth, August 29, 2015.

Michael Hurwitz

1. Jerome Clark, "Michael Hurwitz and the Aimless Drifters," review of *Cowboy Fandango*, Rambles.net, February 9, 2008, www.rambles.net/hurwitz _fandang07.html (accessed February 2008).

Ken Jones

1. Author interview with Ken Jones, September 15, 2015.
2. Ibid.
3. Ibid.

Walt LaRue

1. "Never Forgotten: Walt LaRue," CowboyPoetry .com, www.cowboypoetry.com/sincenews8two2.htm (accessed September 19, 2015).
2. Mark Bedor, "The Art and Ways of Walt LaRue," *Ranch and Reata*, August/September, 2011.
3. Walt LaRue filmography, Internet Movie Database, www.imdb.com/name/nm0479023 (accessed September 19, 2015).
4. Bedor, "Art and Ways."

Chris LeDoux

1. "Chris LeDoux," Texas Trail of Fame, http:// texastrailoffame.org/inductees/chris-ledoux (accessed August 24, 2015).
2. "Chris LeDoux," Wikipedia, https://en.wikipedia. org/wiki/Chris_LeDoux (accessed August 24, 2015).
3. Charlie Seemann, "Chris LeDoux," in *The Encyclopedia of Country Music*, ed. Paul Kingsbury (New York: Oxford UP, 1998), 293.

4. "Chris LeDoux," Wikipedia.
5. Seemann, "Chris LeDoux."
6. "Biography," Chris LeDoux website, www.chris ledoux.com/bio (accessed August 30, 2015).
7. "Chris LeDoux," Wikipedia.
8. "Chris LeDoux Immortalized in Bronze," ChicagoAtHome.com, March 7, 2007, http://archive. is/gCV70 (accessed August 30, 2015).

Daron Little

1. "Daron Little Biography," CD Baby Music Store, www.cdbaby.com/Artist/DaronLittle (accessed August 18, 2015).
2. "Daron Little," FolkAlley.com, www.folkalley.com/ openmic/artist.php?id=1241 (accessed August 25, 2015).
3. As quoted on the Daron Little website, http:// ranchcowboymusic.com/home (accessed August18, 2015).

Corb Lund

1. "Corb Lund Biography," Maple Music, www.maple music.com/artists/cor/bio.asp (accessed August 30, 2015).
2. Ibid.

Gary McMahan

1. "Bio," Gary McMahan website, www.singing cowboy.com (accessed July 22, 2015).
2. "Gary McMahan," Wikipedia, https://en .wikipedia.org/wiki/Gary_McMahan (accessed July 22 2015).

3. "Gary McMahan: Working Cowboy Turned Entertainer," *Western Way*, Winter 2014, www.westernmusic.org/userfiles/WW%20Winter-web.pdf (accessed July 22, 2015).

Chuck Milner

1. "Chuck Milner," CowboyFrank.net, www.cowboyfrank.net/real/albums/Chuck_Milner/bio.htm (accessed October 27, 2015).
2. Ibid.

Rooster Morris

1. "Rooster Morris," Amazon.com author page, www.amazon.com/Rooster-Morris/e/B00368WK6U (accessed November 2, 2015).
2. "Rooster Morris," Wikipedia, https://en.wikipedia.org/wiki/Rooster_Morris (accessed November 2, 2015).
3. "Rooster Morris," Amazon.com author page.

Glenn Ohrlin

1. "Glenn Ohrlin," NEA National Heritage Fellowships, www.arts.gov/honors/heritage/fellows/glenn-ohrlin (accessed March 18, 2016).
2. Ibid.
3. Ibid.

Ken Overcast

1. "A Biography of Ken Overcast," Ken Overcast website, www.kenovercast.com/about-ken (accessed November 4, 2015).

2. "A Life Worth Keeping," America's Horse Daily, December 17, 2012, http://americashorsedaily.com/a-life-worth-keeping/comment-page-1 (accessed November 4, 2015).
3. Author interview with Ken Overcast, November 3, 2015.
4. Author interview, November 3, 2015
5. Author interview.

Howard Parker

1. "Never Forgotten: Howard Parker," CowboyPoetry.com, www.cowboypoetry.com/howardparker.htm (accessed November 8, 2015).

J Parson

1. "About J," J Parson website, www.jparson.com/about (accessed November 9, 2015).
2. Ibid.

Bob Petermann

1. "Featured at the Bar-D Ranch: Bob Petermann," CowboyPoetry.com, www.cowboypoetry.com/bobpetermann.htm (accessed November 11, 2015).
2. "Cowboys Lend Hand to Memorial," *Tribune* (New Hampton, IA), January 31, 2013, www.nhtrib.com/news/article_8650836a-6bc8-11e2-8ace-001a4bcf887a.html (accessed March 14, 2016).

Jean and Gary Prescott

1. "Featured at the Bar-D Ranch: Jean Prescott," CowboyPoetry.com, www.cowboypoetry.com/jeanprescott.htm (accessed March 19, 2016).

Buck Ramsey

1. All text and quotes in this entry from Charlie Seemann and Bette Ramsey, liner notes to *Buck Ramsey: Hittin' the Trail*, Smithsonian Folkways Recordings, http://media.smithsonianfolkways.org/liner_notes/smithsonian_folkways/SFW50002.pdf (accessed March 16, 2015).

Luke Reed

1. Author interview with Luke Reed, November 18, 2015.
2. Ibid.

Ray Reed

1. Ray Reed Obituary, *Ruidoso News*, February 6, 1998.
2. Ibid.

Brigid Reedy

1. "Brigid Reedy," 31st National Cowboy Poetry Gathering, http://31stnationalcowboypoetrygat 2015.sched.org/volunteer/brigidreedy (accessed November 20, 2015).
2. "Brigid Reedy," CowboyPoetry.com, www.cowboy poetry.com/brigidreedy.htm (accessed November 20, 2015).
3. "Young Yodeler Brings Experience, Excitement to Gathering," *Elko Daily Free Press*, January 28, 2014, http://elkodaily.com/lifestyles/young-yodeler -brings-experience-excitement-to-gathering/ article_76df8284-8867-11e3-9183-0019bb2963f4 .html (accessed November 20, 2015).

Dave Schildt

1. Author interview, November 25, 2015

Trinity Seely

1. Tom Moates, "Meet Trinity Seely," *Eclectic Horseman*, September 15, 2014, http:// eclectic-horseman.com/meet-trinity-seely (accessed December 8, 2015).

Clyde Sproat

1. "Clyde 'Kindy' Sproat," NEA National Heritage Fellowships, www.arts.gov/honors/heritage/fellows/ clyde-kindy-sproat (accessed November 21, 2015).
2. Ibid.
3. Ibid.

Dave Stamey

1. Terry Roland, "Dave Stamey: Cowboy Songs Are Alive and Well," *San Diego Troubadour*, January 2002, http://sandiegotroubadour.com/2012/01/ dave-stamey-cowboy-songs-are-alive-and-well (accessed March 14, 2016).

Gail Steiger

1. Author interview with Gail Steiger, June 22, 2014.
2. Ibid.

Linda Svendsen

1. Author interview with Linda Svendsen, October 15, 2015.
2. Ibid.

Caitlyn Taussig

1. Author interview with Caitlyn Taussig, December 15, 2015.
2. Ibid.

Rod Taylor

1. Rod Taylor, *Here, There, Anywhere* album notes, CD Baby Music Store, www.cdbaby.com/cd/RodTaylor (accessed December 19, 2015).
2. David Bowser, "Philmont Hand Finds Horizons Expanding in Many Directions," *Livestock Weekly*, October 23, 1997, www.livestockweekly.com/papers/97/10/23/whltaylor.asp (accessed November 7, 2015).

Ian Tyson

1. "Ian Tyson," Wikipedia, https://en.wikipedia.org/wiki/Ian Tyson (accessed December 2, 2015).
2. "Ian Tyson Biography," iTunes, https://itunes.apple.com/ca/artist/ian-tyson/id534433 (accessed December 2, 2015).
3. Ian Tyson, *The Long Trail: My Life in the West* (Toronto: Random House Canada, 2010), 87-95.
4. "Ian Tyson," Wikipedia.

Jessie Veeder

1. "About Jessie Veeder and the Veeder Ranch," Meanwhile, Back at the Ranch . . ., http://veeder ranch.com/about (accessed March 19, 2016).
2. "Jessie Veeder Biography," Sonicbids, www.sonic bids.com/band/jessieveeder (accessed December 9, 2015).
3. "Jessie Veeder," Bush Foundation, www.bush foundation.org/about-us/bio/jessie-veeder (accessed December 9, 2015).

Hub Whitt

1. Author interview with Hub Whitt, October 15, 2015.
2. Ibid.
3. Ibid.
4. Ibid.

INDEX

ART AND PHOTO CREDITS

Front Matter
p. i: *A Fine Old Martin* by William Matthews

Jesse Ballantyne
p. 9: Kevin Martini-Fuller

Mike Beck
p. 11: Kevin Martini-Fuller
p. 12: Sanne Lykkegaard Wiesneck,
p. 13: Mike Beck

Adrian Brannan
p. 14: Adrian Brannan
p. 15: Jessica Brandi Lifland

Dale Burson and Family
pp. 16 and 17: Becki Burson

Lyle Cunningham
p. 19: Kevin Martini-Fuller

Jay Dalton
pp. 21 and 22: Diane Dalton

Kevin Davis
p. 24: Sheri Davis
p. 25: Zane Davis

Stephanie Davis
p. 27: Jessica Brandi Lifland
p. 28: Charlie Ekburg
p. 29: Rick Phillip

Geno Delafose
p. 31: Jessica Brandi Lifland

Duane Dickinson
p. 33: Duane Dickinson

Juni Fisher
p. 35: Kit Cramer
p. 36: Marie Geibel

Brownie Ford
pp. 39 and 40: Nick Spitzer

Ryan Fritz
p. 43: Ryan Fritz
p. 44: Patricia Brewer

Gillette Brothers
p. 47: Ross Hecox and *Western Horseman*
p. 48: Kevin Martini-Fuller
p. 49: Guy Gillette

D. W. Groethe
pp. 51 and 52: Jessica Brandi Lifland

Wylie Gustafson
p. 54: Colleen Gustafson
p. 55: Bill Watts

Kenny Hall
p. 57: Charlie Ekburg

Luke Reed
p. 120: Chisholm Trail Heritage Center

Ray Reed
p. 123: Natalie Brown Baca

Brigid Reedy
pp. 124 and 125: John Michael Reedy

Dave Schildt
p. 126: David Schildt
p. 127: Chris Simon

Trinity Seely
p. 128: Jennifer Denison
p. 129: Charlie Ekburg

Clyde Sproat
p. 131: Cheryl Sproat
p. 132: Lynn Martin Graton

Dave Stamey
p. 134: Sheila Varian
p. 135: Jeremy Ball/Bottle Branding

Gail Steiger
pp. 137 and 139: Steve Atkinson
p. 138: Charlie Seemann

T. R. Stewart
pp. 140 and 142: Mindy Millers

Linda Svendsen
pp. 144 and 145: Linda Svendsen

Caitlyn Taussig
pp. 146 and 148: Jennifer Denison and *Western Horseman* magazine
p. 147: Jessica Brandi Lifland

Rod Taylor
p. 150: Jessica Brandi Lifland
p. 151: Ann L. Wilson
p. 152: Larry D. Walker

Ian Tyson
p. 154: S. Lee Gunderson
p. 155: Kevin Martini-Fuller

Jessie Veeder
p. 158: Jessica Brandi Lifland
p. 159: Jessie Veeder

Johnny Whelan
p. 161: Natalie Brown Baca

Hub Whitt
pp. 163 and 164: Hub Whitt

ABOUT THE AUTHOR

Charlie Seemann is the executive director emeritus of the Western Folklife Center in Elko, Nevada. He holds an MA in folklife studies from the University of California at Los Angeles. He was an instructor in folklore and folk music at Moorpark College in California for six years, and then he worked as a folklorist and director of the Western Regional Folklife Festival for the National Park Service/Golden Gate National Recreation Area in San Francisco until 1981. He then moved to Nashville, Tennessee, where he was deputy director at the Country Music Foundation/Country Music Hall of Fame for twelve years. He served as program director of the Fund for Folk Culture in Santa Fe, New Mexico, before assuming the executive director position at the Western Folklife Center in 1998. He retired in 2014.

CARVING
DESPERADOS
with Tom Wolfe

Text written with and photography
by Douglas Congdon-Martin

Schiffer Publishing Ltd

77 Lower Valley Road, Atglen, PA 19310

Contents

**Library of Congress
Cataloging-in-Publication Data**

Wolfe, Tom (Tom James)
 Carving desperados with Tom Wolfe/text
written with and photography by Douglas
Congdon-Martin.
  p. cm.
 ISBN 0-7643-0097-0 (paper)
 1. Wood-carving. 2. Wood-carved figurines-
-Caricatures and cartoons. 3. Busts--Caricatures
and cartoons. I. Congdon-Martin, Douglas. II.
Title.
TT199.7.W6424 1996
736'.4--dc20   96-13640
                          CIP

Printed in China

ISBN: 0-7643-0097-0

Published by Schiffer Publishing, Ltd.
77 Lower Valley Road
Atglen, PA 19310
Please write for a free catalog.
This book may be purchased from the publisher.
Please include $2.95 postage.
Try your bookstore first.

We are interested in hearing from authors
with book ideas on related subjects.

Introduction

Some of you may have already guessed that I love to carve. I've carved most everything you can imagine, from dragons to rats, Santas to Woodspirits, and everytime I pick up the knife it is with a sense of anticipation. Something interesting is going to happen!

Of all the things I carve, faces give me the most pleasure. Out of a formless block of wood a full-blown personality emerges. It has an attitude, emotions, and a story to tell. It can be happy or sad, serious or funny, smart or dumb, heroic or common, honest or conniving. And all of this because of the way I carve it. It never ceases to amaze me how changing the angle of the eyes or the shape of the mouth speaks volumes about the character I am carving.

Because I love to carve faces, I spend a lot of time carving busts of people. They can be different sizes and shapes, but generally I like to make them about 8 inches tall. This gives me enough room to do detailed work. Most often I carve them in two pieces, the head and the base. This permits me to change positions of the head until I get the effect I most want.

I hope you enjoy these as much as I have. Good luck!

Papa Maynot

Carving the Bust

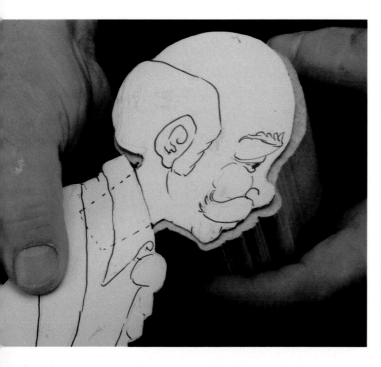

Cut the blank for the head from 2-1/2 to 3 inch stock. I am using basswood.

Because there is no hat, I can knock off the corner of the head with the saw. Draw a line about 1/2" from the outer edge, put the bandsaw table at a 45 degree angle and cut on the line.

On the front draw the line of the neck. This is done free hand. The base is as wide as the wood is thick and it tapers out at the jaw. You can saw it on the bandsaw or, if you do not have one available, you can carve it away.

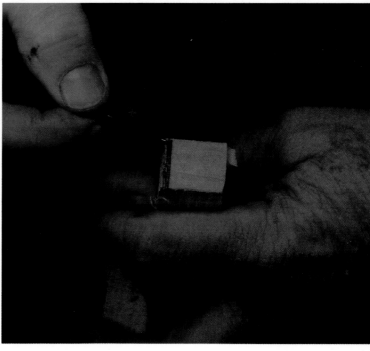

Make any adjustments needed to make the bottom of the neck square.

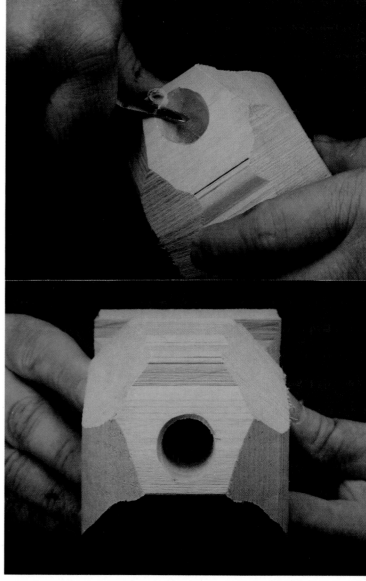

The base was cut from a board that is 4" thick, but I found a hard drying spot on one edge, so I'm going to take a little bit off each side. The neck hole is centered and measures 3/4" in diameter.

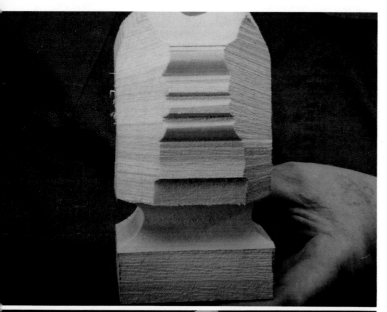

Lightly bevel the opening of the neck. This will make the neck appear to go under the collar.

Rough cuts can be done on the bandsaw, setting the front view, and knocking off the front corners. This saves a lot of carving time and energy.

Returning to the head, knock off the corners of the neck to take it to octagonal.

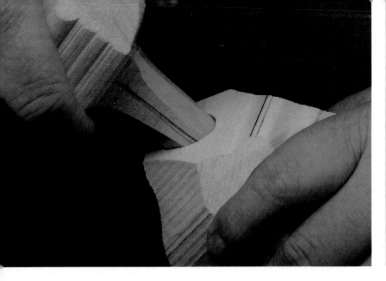

Push the neck into the body and rotate it under pressure.

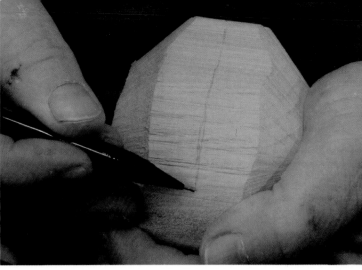

Draw a center line all the way around the head.

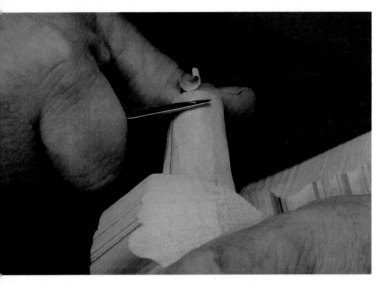

This will create shiny spots where the high points are so you can shave them off.

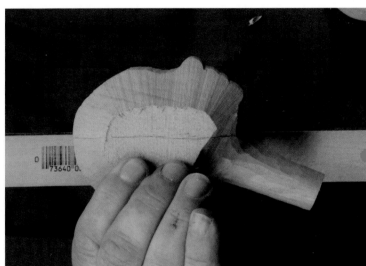

When looking at the side of the head, the center line does not run with the neck. Rather it sort of goes from the Adam's apple to the crown of the scalp as you can see in this picture. Draw the center line.

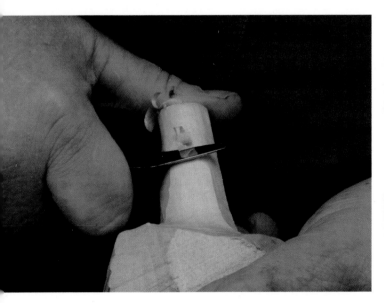

When the end is set carve the rest of the neck so it gradually slopes down to it.

The bottom of the ear is defined by a line running from the bottom of the nose to the nape of the neck.

The top of the ear is on a line running parallel to the last one and coming back from the center of the eye.

Continue shaping the top of the head.

The ear fits in this box.

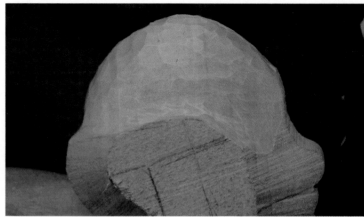

The head shaped.

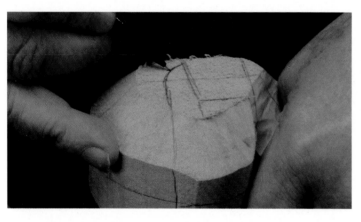

Draw in the hair line of this bald gentleman.

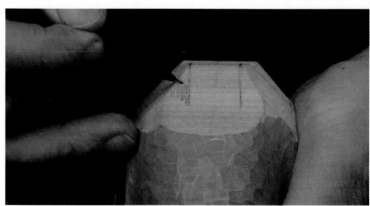

Mark the width of the nose, leaving it wide for now.

To shape the skull, come up from the hairline with a scooping cut.

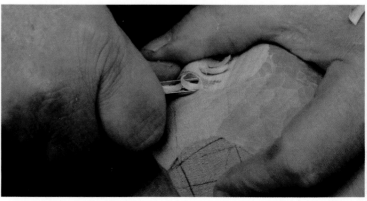

Use a gouge to remove the sides of the nose. This leaves a nice smooth line beside the nose.

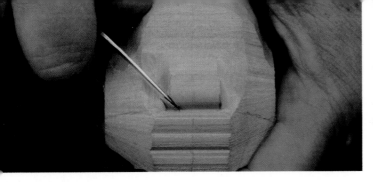

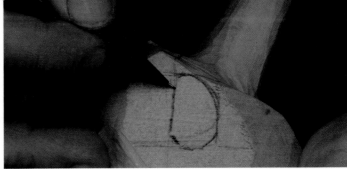

Knock off the bottom corners of the nose. This helps create the "button" of the nose tip.

Draw in the ear.

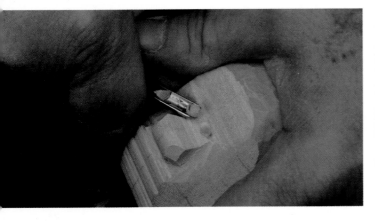

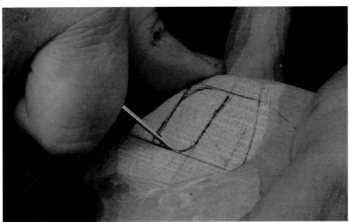

With a gouge cut a channel along the side of the nose, angling up toward the bridge.

Cut a stop around the ear. Go lightly at the top so the hair can come almost over it.

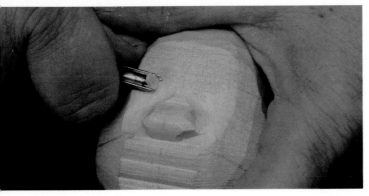

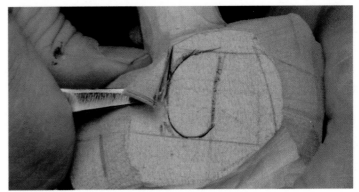

Gouge out the eye socket.

Cut back to the stop, taking a good bit off right behind the ear.

Progress.

At the bottom of the ear use a gouge to make a sweeping cut to the neck.

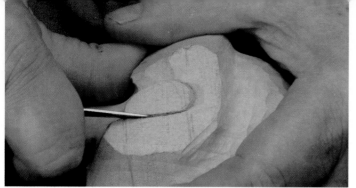

Cut a stop on the back line of the sideburns.

Gouge a channel from the temple into the eyesocket.

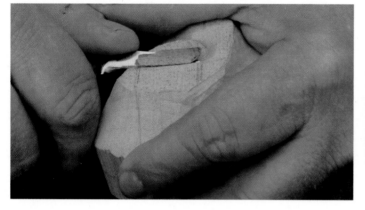

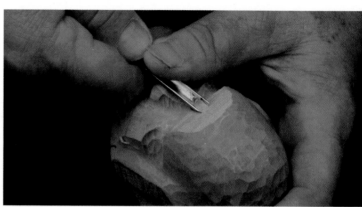

Make a slanting cut from the rim of the ear back to the stop.

Create a little separation between the eyebrows.

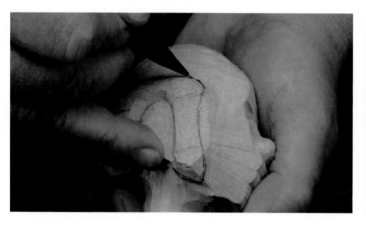

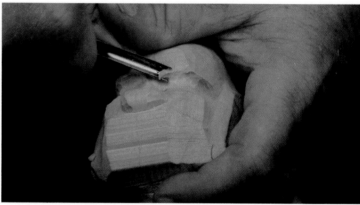

I want a nice bushy sideburn, so I draw it in an exaggerated way.

Add a little lift to the eyebrows with the gouge.

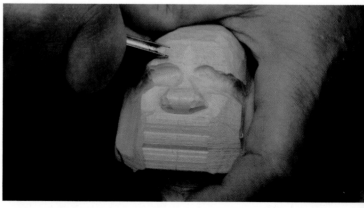

Make a scooping cut from the sideburn into the jaw.

Cut a channel over the eyebrows.

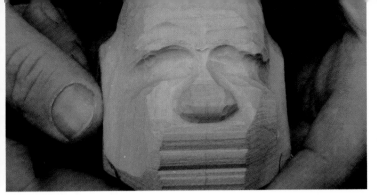

Progress.

and up along the surface of the lip..

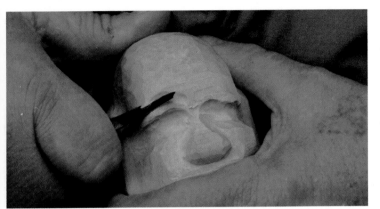

Clean up the carving, blending the gouge lines into the surfaces.

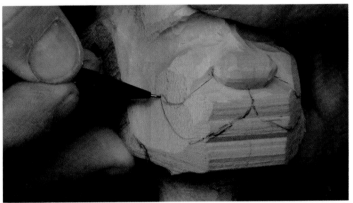

Draw in the moustache.

Cut a stop beside the nose.

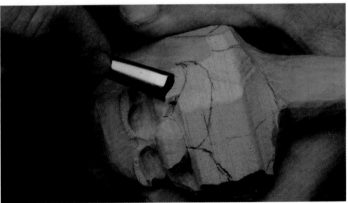

With the cup of the gouge against the cheek, cut down to the moustache.

Cut down along the surface of the cheek...

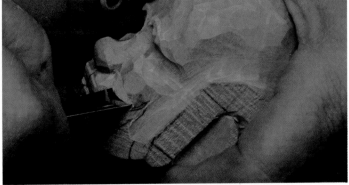

With the same gouge, cup side up, cut straight in on the line of the moustache to cut off the shaving.

Where the moustache separates, cut a stop in each line and back to them from below to pop out a nitch.

Gouge a channel under the bottom lip.

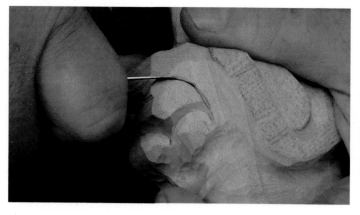

Cut a stop along the lower edge of the moustache.

Progress.

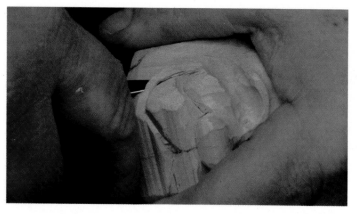

Slice back the stop from the jaw.

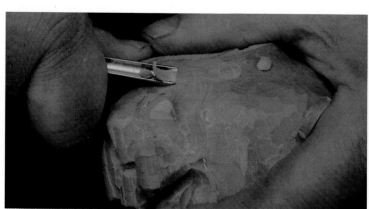

With a gouge, strengthen the line between the face and sideburns.

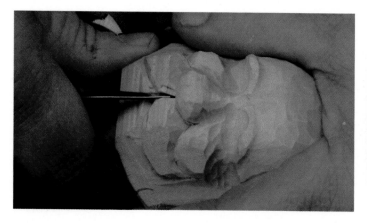

Separate between the two sides of the moustache.

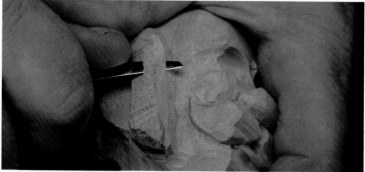

There is a little bit too much thickness to the sideburns and it's getting in the way. To fix this I'm going to bevel the surface of the sideburn out from the cheek.

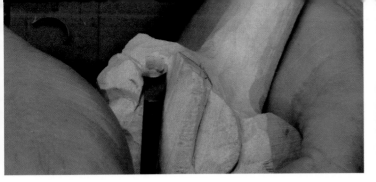

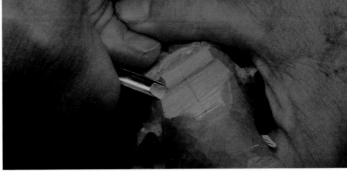

Gouging between the moustache and the sideburn gives the cheek a natural sunken look.

With a gouge, narrow the chin from both sides.

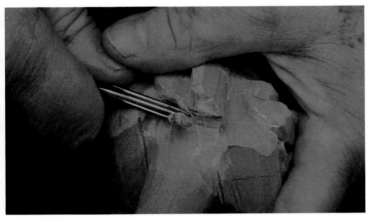

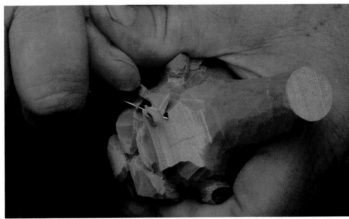

With a veiner undercut the bottom of the ear and the end of the sideburn. This will make the sideburn look like its hanging past the jaw.

After it is narrowed, round it off and make it believable.

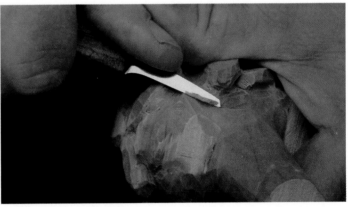

Clean things up with a knife.

The strong jaw this guy has is out of character, so I need to reduce it a little.

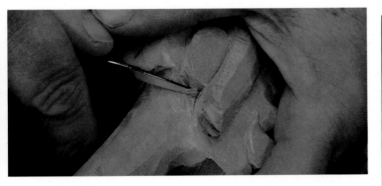

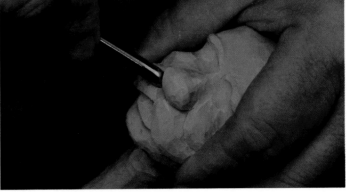

Cut a nitch at the bottom of the ear to define the boundary with the sideburn. I always try to have the sideburn hang well below the end of ear or well above it, but never at the same level. That would make the carving less interesting.

With a half round gouge push straight in to the nostrils.

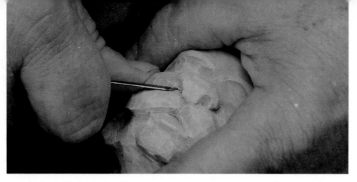

Clip off the chip with a knife.

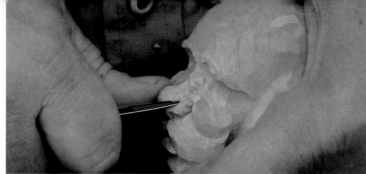

Finish it up with a knife.

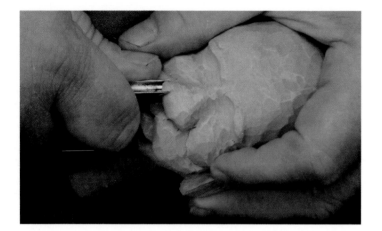

With a gouge cut a channel up and over the nostril flange...

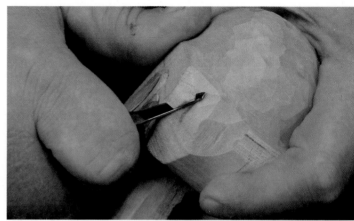

Shape the hair.

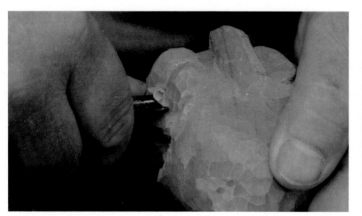

back to the cheek.

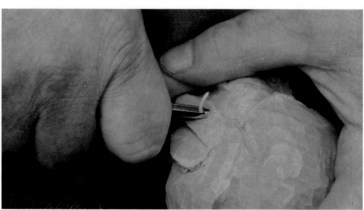

Add hair lines with a big veiner. On the sideburns the lines start at the ear and move up to the front edge in an s-shape.

The nose is ready for rounding.

The lines of the hair also sweep back from the face with a slight wave.

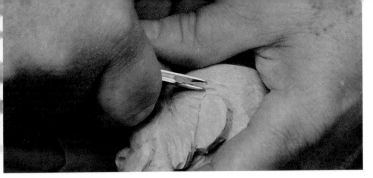

Add a few finer lines with a small veiner.

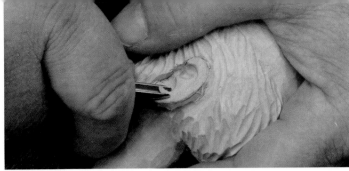

A third groove goes around the inside of the rim.

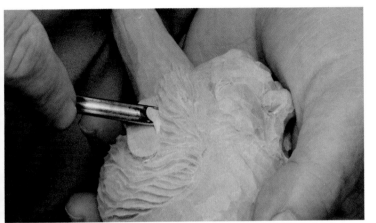

The inside of the ear is basically two grooves. The bottom groove goes straight from the rim to the front edge.

Round off the outside edge of the ear.

The upper groove follows the rim and turns into the front edge above the first groove.

The result.

Cut of the shaving with a knife.

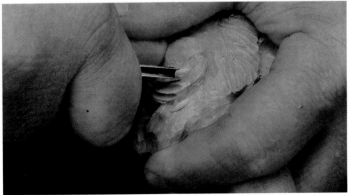

With the big veiner carve the lines of the moustache so they flow naturally.

Switch to a smaller veiner to get closer to the nose.

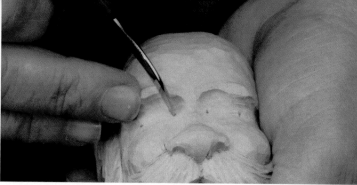

At the inside dot push your knife in at a 45 degree angle above...

At the bridge of the nose make a dot equal distances from the center to mark the inside of the eye.

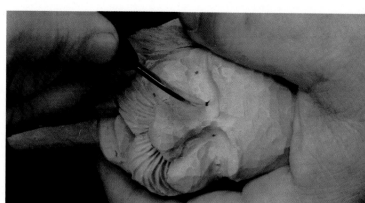

and below.

Make another dot about the same distance apart to mark the outside of the eye. Do the same on the other side.

With the point of the knife, knock out the angle created by those two cuts.

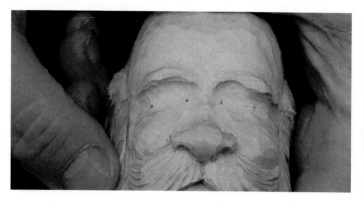

The dots in place.

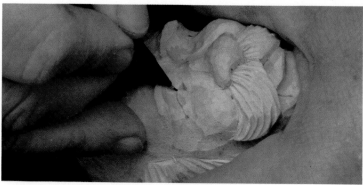

From the outside point, draw a line to the end of the top angle cut. This line should curve a little in the middle.

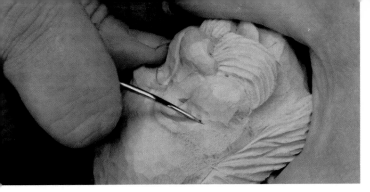

At the corner push you knife straight in so it follows the line you drew.

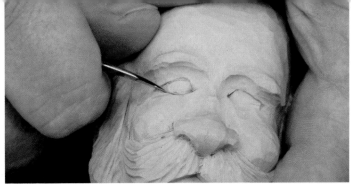

Cut stops along the top and bottom lines to connect one side to the other.

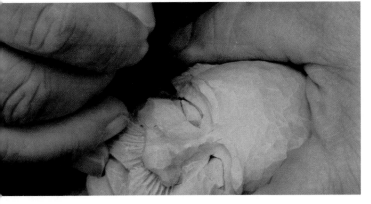

Draw the bottom line.

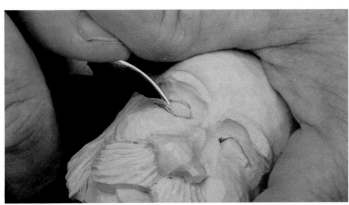

Cut from the eyeball back to the stops, rounding the eyeball.

Push your knife straight in at the outside corner again, aligning the blade with the bottom line.

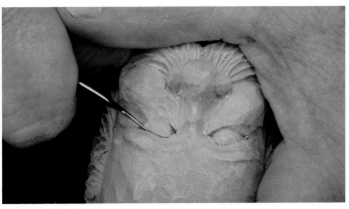

Repeat on the other side.

Come into the corner to pop out the nitch.

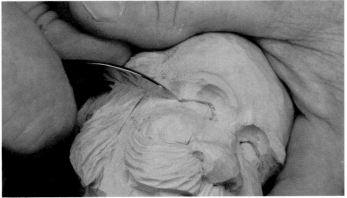

Extend the line of the top lid out a little beyond the corner...

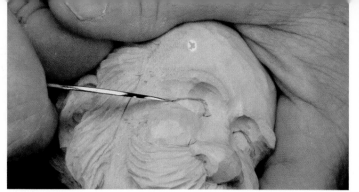

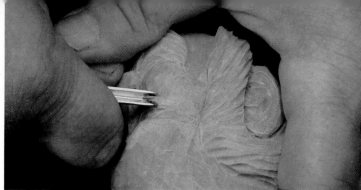

and cut back to it from the bottom. This creates a little crow's foot, making the eye look bigger while bringing the lower lid under the upper.

Return to the middle and cut outward.

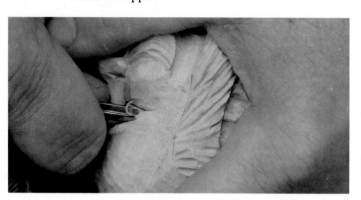

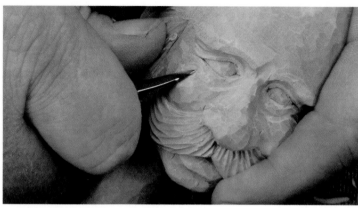

To shape the upper eyelid, start above the eye in the middle with a veiner and run it to the outside.

Soften the lower line with a knife.

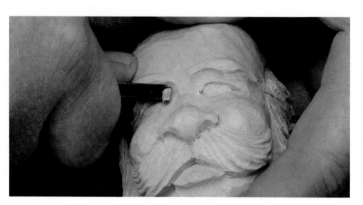

Return to the middle and go toward the nose, letting the cut fade out.

With a veiner add hairlines to the eyebrows.

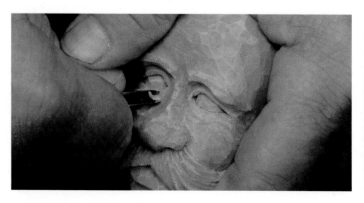

Do the same thing underneath, starting in the middle and going toward the nose.

The eye area finished.

I often clean up areas as I go, like here on the head.

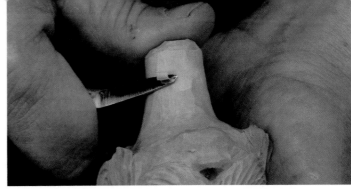

Trim away the shiny spots created by the rotation.

I think this guy would like a good smoke, so I'm going to cut a place for a cigar in the middle of his mouth.

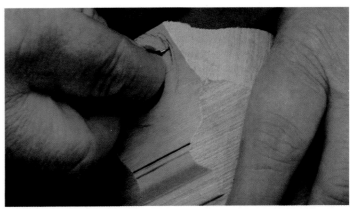

Mark an area around the collar. This is a "no-carve" area that acts as a safety.

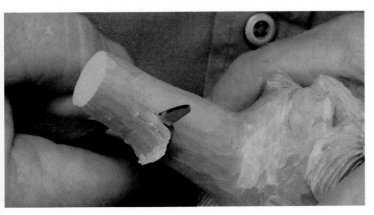

In preparation for the final fitting of the head in the body, trim an inch off the end of the neck.

Round off the corners to bring the collar down to the size of the line.

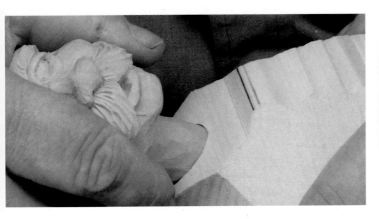

Refit the neck by pushing it into its socket and rotating it.

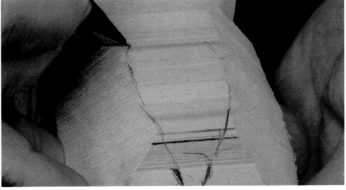

The shirtfront will be ruffled. I'm drawing lines to make sure I don't carve it until I'm ready.

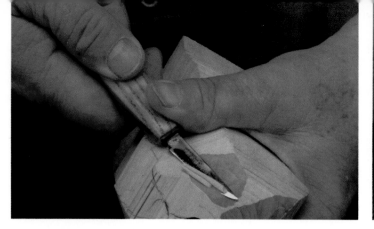

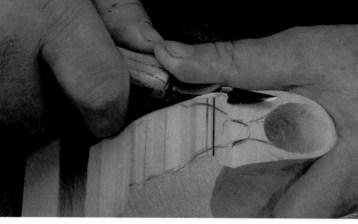

This tool position provides a lot of power and control. The hand holding the tool keeps the knife in contact with the wood and provides a fulcrum, while the thumb of the other hand pushes the blade through the wood. Use it to round the front of the shoulders.

and cut back to it from the collar. The ruffle will stick out in front.

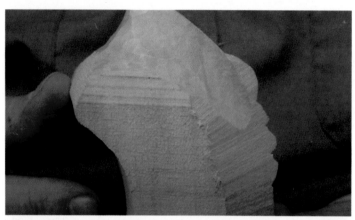

Continue down the side of the ruffle.

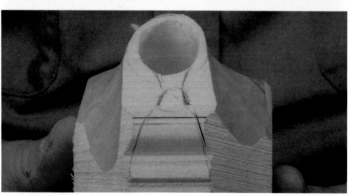

Progress. This figure will have a high collar.

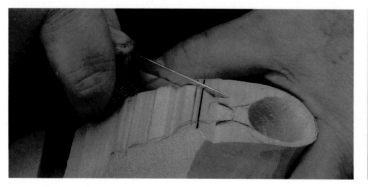

Cut a stop in the side of the ruffle...

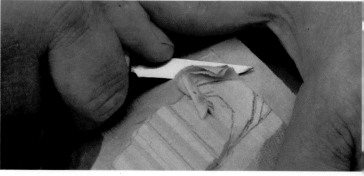

Draw the lines of the ruffle to continue down the front.

Cut a stop and trim back to it.

Open up the front of the collar just a little.

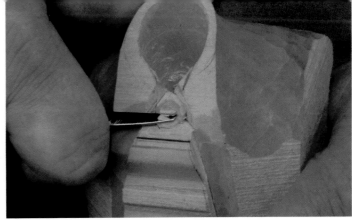

Reduce the surface of the knot.

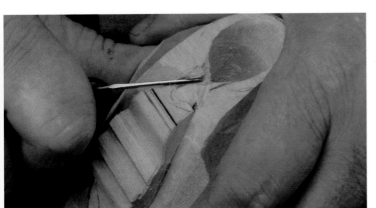

Cut around the knot at the top of the ruffle.

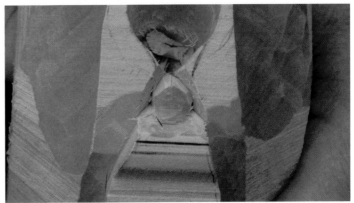

The result.

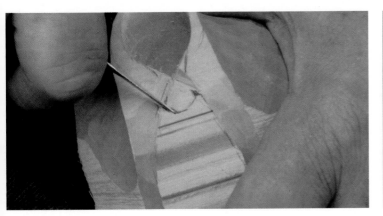

At the corner of the knot cut in on the line...

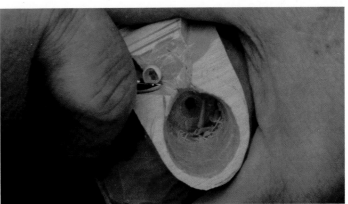

With a gouge, undercut the front of the collar.

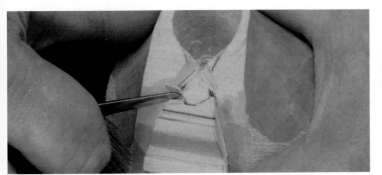

and back to it from the ruffle to knock out a nitch that defines the lower corners of the knot.

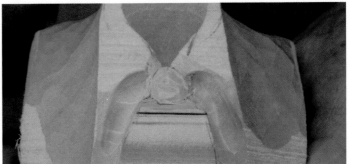

Progress.

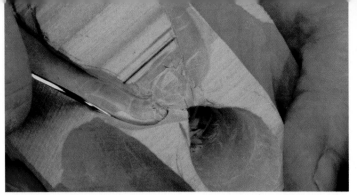

Sharpen the line of the edge of the collar with a knife.

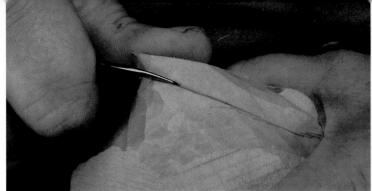

The collar rolls up in the back revealing a little of the back of the ruffle. Cut a stop in the line of the collar.

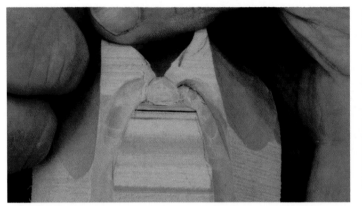

With one side done you can see how much more believable it is.

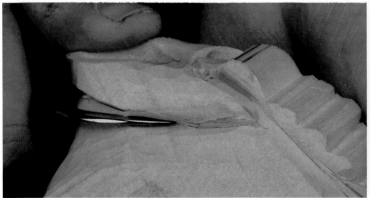

Trim back to it from below.

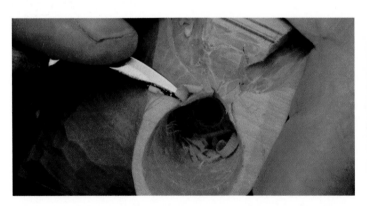

Round over the surface of the collar.

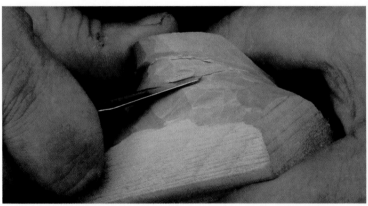

Cut a stop in the line of the scarf at the back of the neck, and trim back to it from the shoulders.

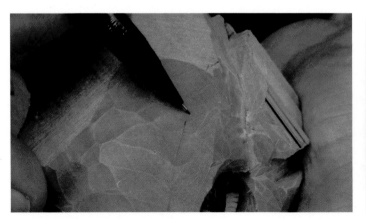

Draw in the bottom edge of the collar.

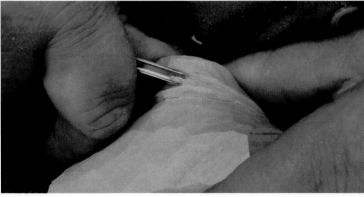

With a veiner add some folds to the back of the ruffled scarf.

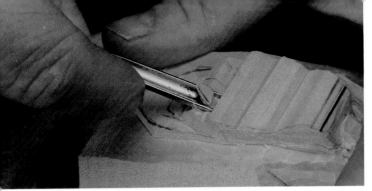

At the lowest fold of the ruffle begin by running the gouge up one side, slightly in from the edge. Go to the top of the fold.

This leaves a raised portion in between. On the bottom edge of this push straight in with the gouge, cup side down.

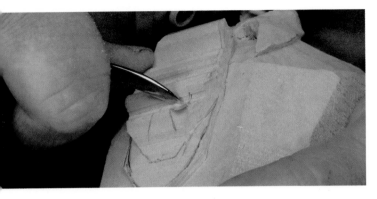

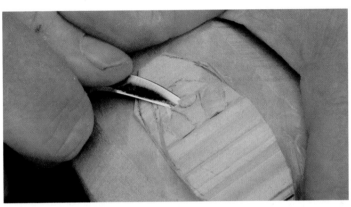

Clip of the shaving with a knife.

Clip off the half-moon this forms.

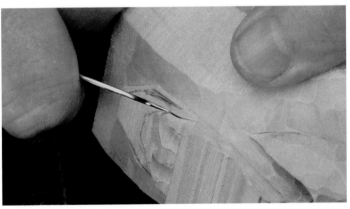

Do the same on the other side, up the fold...

On the edge of the ruffle we need to undercut. Cut a slightly curved stop...

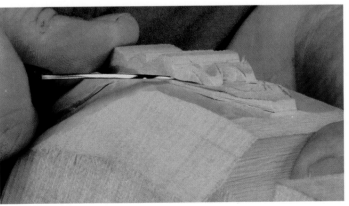

and clip it off.

and clip it off flush with the chest.

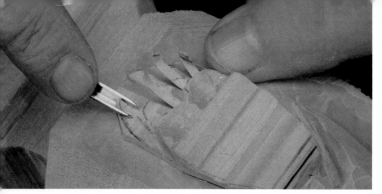

From the bottom of the ruffle run grooves up to the first fold.

Clip off the shaving.

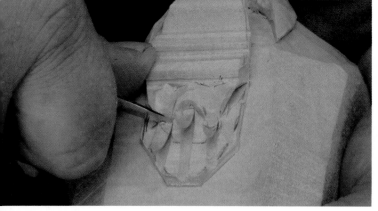

Clip off the shavings at the edge of the first fold.

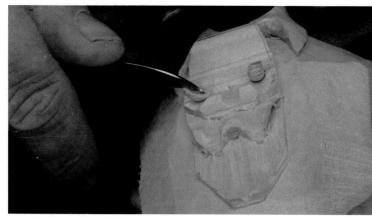

Two more grooves complete the fold.

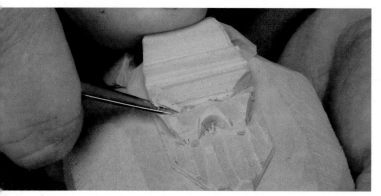

Knock off the corners of the second fold.

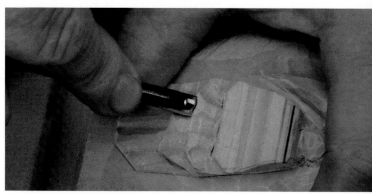

Undercut the raised pleats by pushing straight in with a gouge.

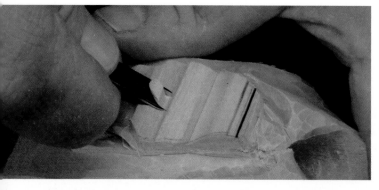

Cut a groove in the middle of the second fold. You want to stagger things so two consecutive folds don't have the same groove pattern.

Clip off the remains.

In the same way undercut the highpoints of the lower section of the scarf to break up the line.

Cut a stop around the line of the vest.

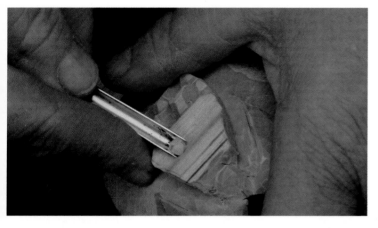

The top two folds are also carved this way...

Trim back to it from the shirt.

Knock off the back upper corners of the bust.

for this result. I've drawn the lines of the vest.

Round and blend them in with the shoulders.

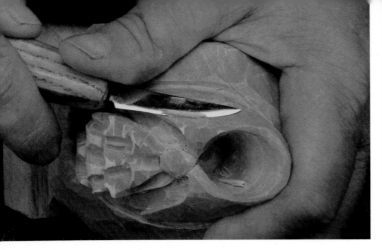

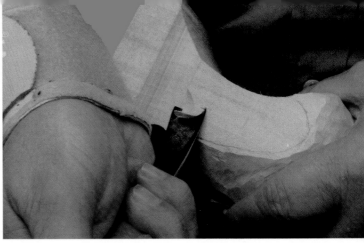

Go over the piece and look for places that don't seem just right. Here I think the collar needs more roll, which I give it with a scooping knife cut.

Working back from the line, gouge the side with a scooping cut.

The portion of the neck piece that goes under the collar should show beside the knot. Cut a stop and trim back to it from the shirt.

Finishing with a flatter gouge will clean up the cut marks.

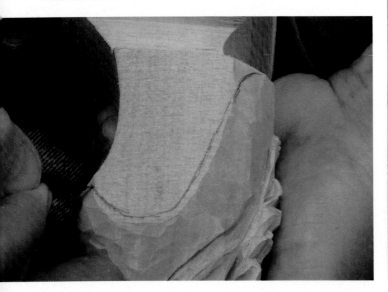

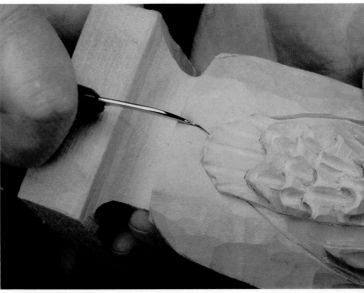

For finishing I want the bottom corner of the vest to turn in and the line to come up to the shoulder seam.

To break up the bottom of the vest I'm going to make the closure and a button. Cut a stop in the closure...

and trim back to it.

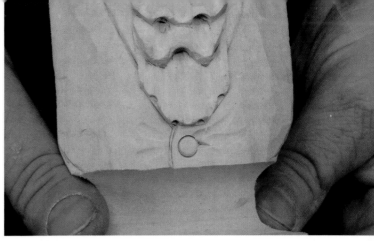

A little triangle at the side for the button hole and the front is finished.

Press and turn an eyepunch or nailset to create the button.

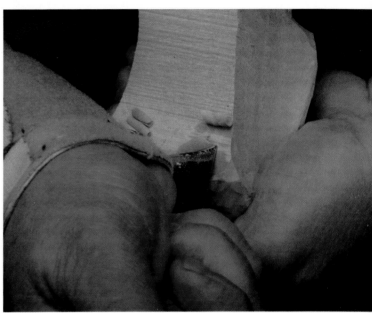

Clean up the back by removing the saw marks.

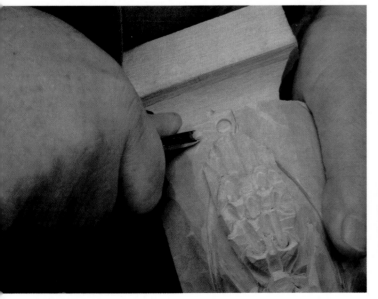

A few stress lines radiating out from the button are made with the gouge.

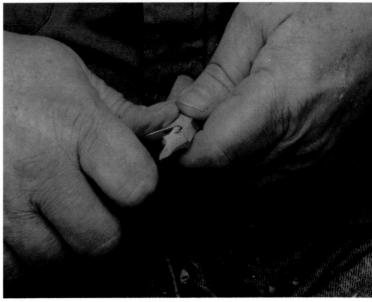

Carve a cigar and holder from a piece of scrap.

Ready for painting.

Painting the Bust

For wood carving I use Winsor and Newton Alkyd tube paints. For most coats the paints are thinned with pure turpentine to a consistency that soaks into the carving, giving subtle colors. What I look for is a watery mixture, almost like a wash. In this way the turpentine will carry the pigment into the wood, giving the stained look I like. It has always been my theory that if you are going to cover the wood, why use wood in the first place? It should be noted that with white, the concentration of the pigment should be a little stronger. I use some pigments right from the tube to add some dry brushed highlight colors.

I mix my paints in juice bottles, putting in a bit of paint and adding turpentine. I don't use exact measurements. Instead I use trial and error, adding a bit of paint or a bit of turpentine until I get the thickness I want.

The juice bottles are handy for holding your paints. They are reclosable, easy to shake, and have the added advantage of leaving a concentrated amount of color on the inside of the lid and the sides of the bottle which can be used when more intense color is needed.

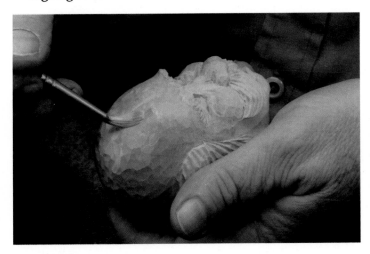

Paint the skin with a flesh tone paint. Mine is a mixture of white, raw sienna, and a touch of pink.

Continue with the blush on the lips and chin.

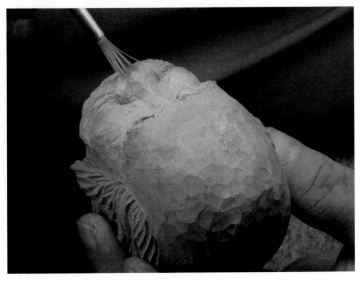

Add a blush of red to tip of the nose, the cheeks, and the forehead, blending it in as you go.

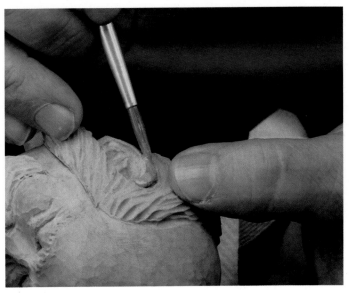

Add a touch more to the tips of the ears.

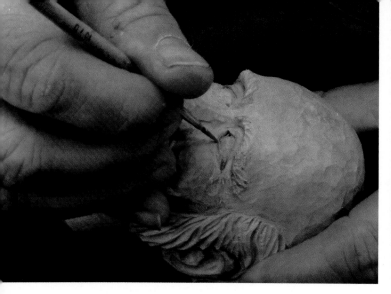

A fine line of the blush red goes around the eyes.

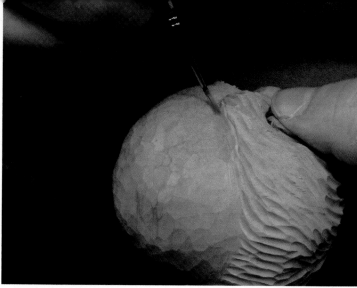

Mixed with flesh color, the burnt sienna creates a soft effect around the hair line...

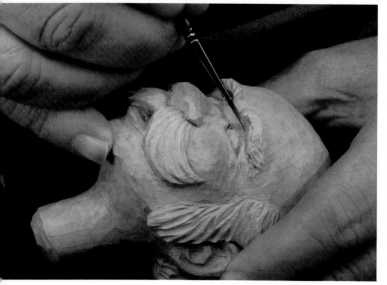

With diluted burnt sienna, add some shading under the eyebrow...

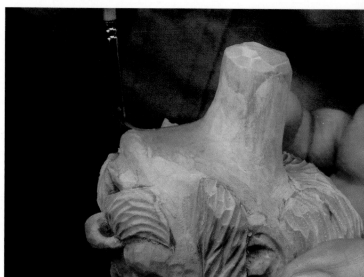

and under the chin.

and in all the shadowy places, like this lower edge of the cheek.

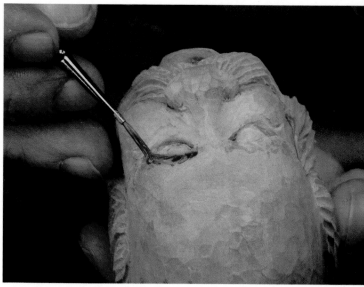

Burnt sienna is the under-color of the hair.

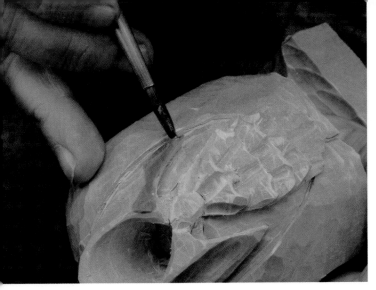

The shirt will be a light blue.

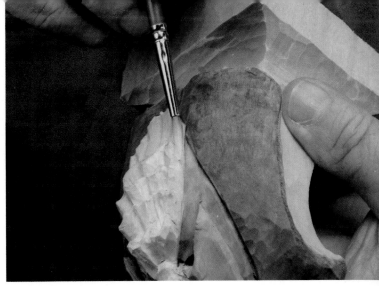

Paint the scarf white.

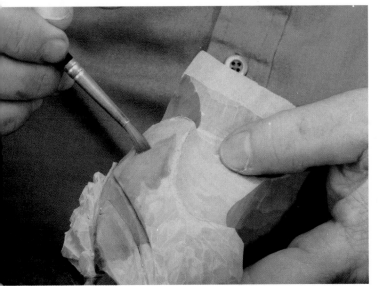

The same blue will be an undercoat on the vest.

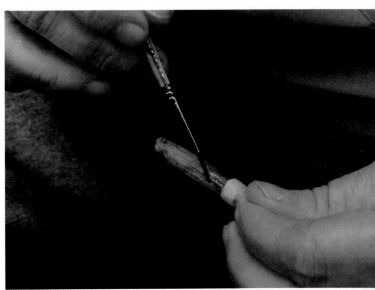

Paint the body of the cigar burnt sienna.

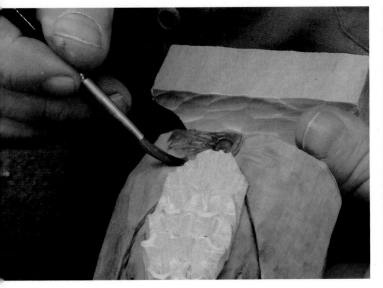

Go over the vest with Alizarin red. With the blue underneath, this forms a plum color.

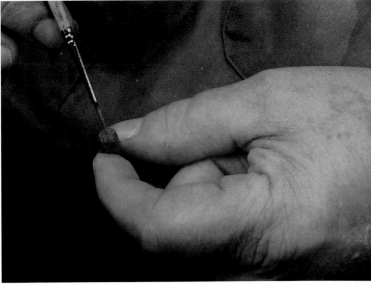

The end is painted red.

The holder is black...

Undercoat the iris with a dark blue.

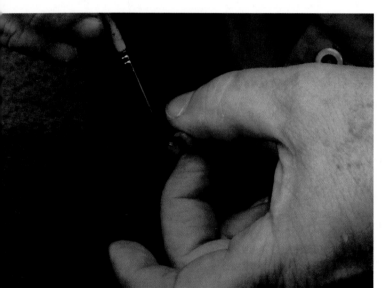

as is the undercoat of the ash.

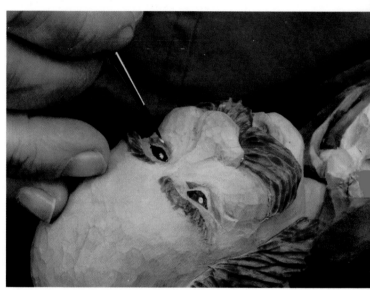

Add a spot of white to each iris...

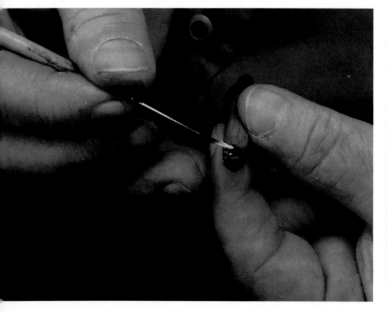

Add some white dots to the ash.

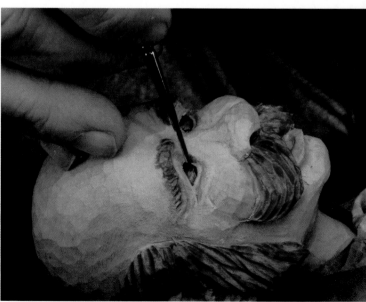

and blend it in to lighten the blue.

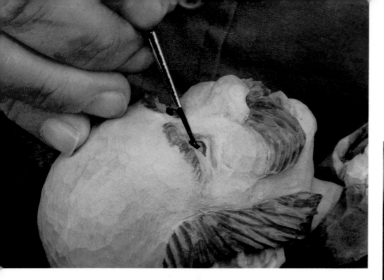

With black add a pupil to each eye.

Add a white speck to the same position in each eye. This is a small spot, so I'm using a bamboo skewer to apply the paint.

Work tube paint into a brush and then brush it out so each individual hair is covered instead of loading the whole brush.

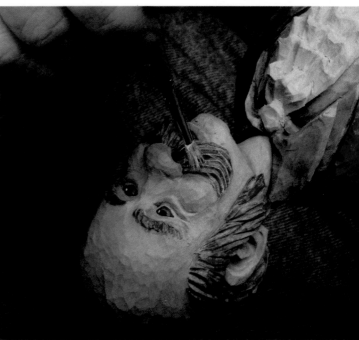

Brush lightly over the hair so the high points pick up the white pigment.

The result.

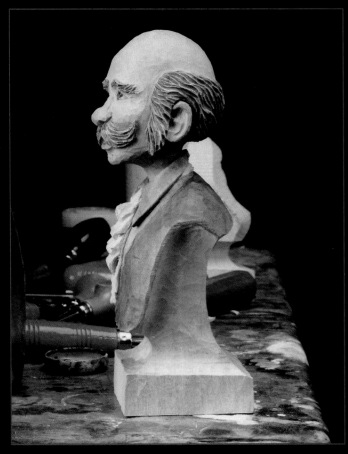

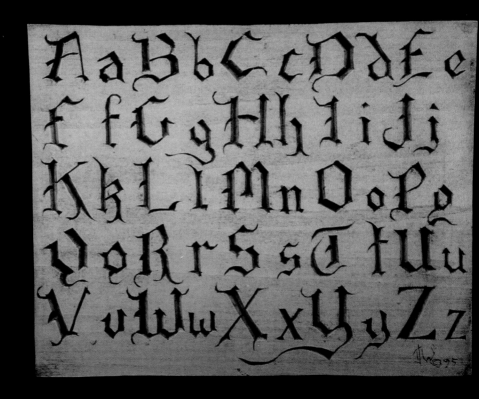

As you will see in the gallery, I often carve the name of the figure in the base. This modified Old English alphabet looks great, and is relatively easy to carve.

Big Nose Rose

Mama May

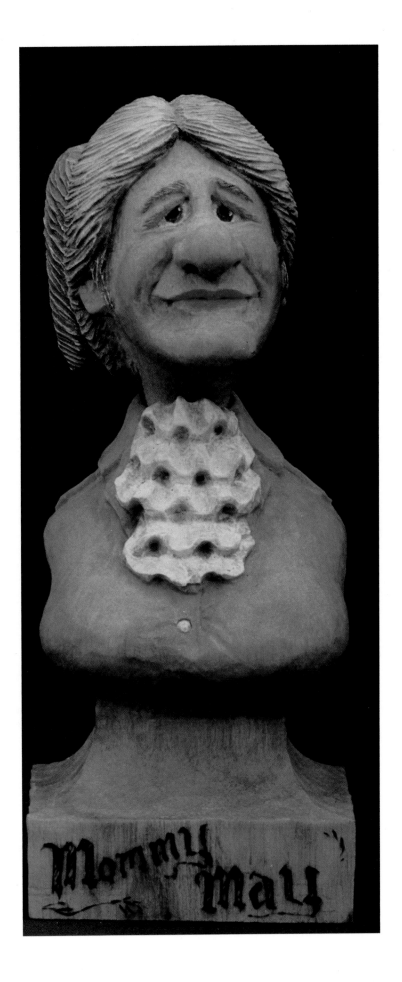

Ace Check A. Lock

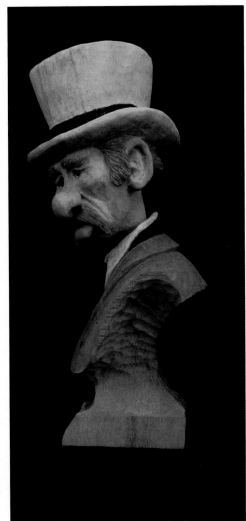

44

Mickey Finn

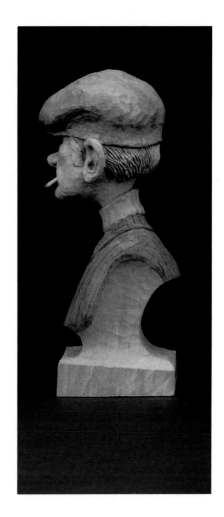

Sexy Sue

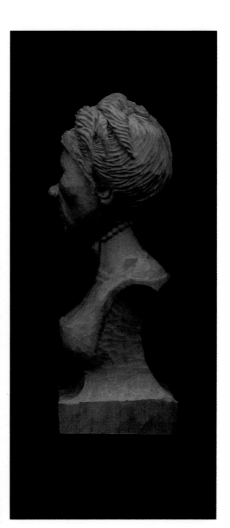

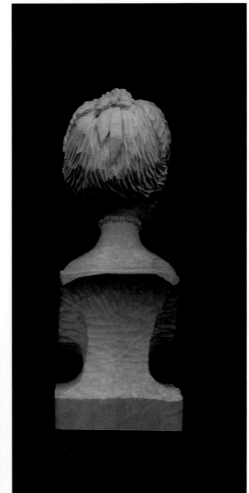

"Little Will" the Scott

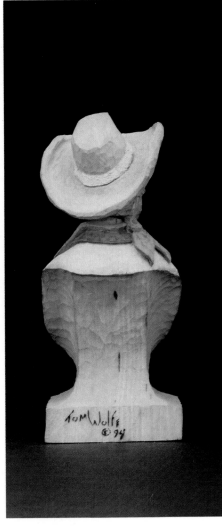

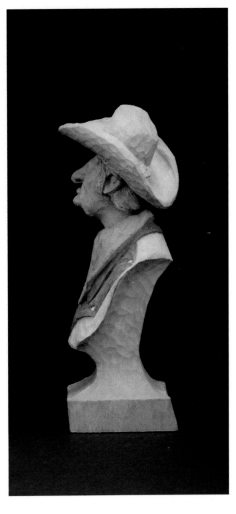

"Little Will" The Scott

50

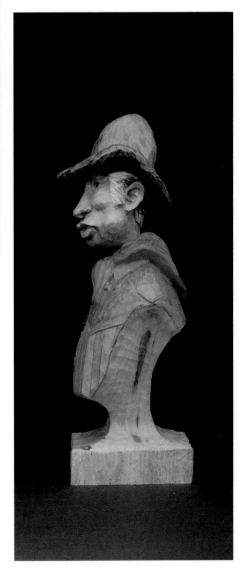

Jim Montana "The Breed"

"Sippen Sid"

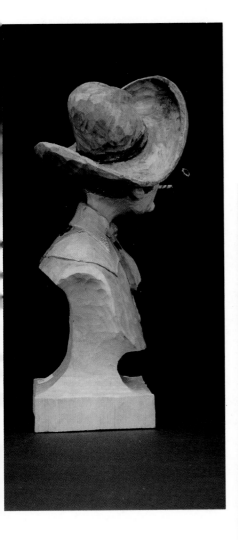

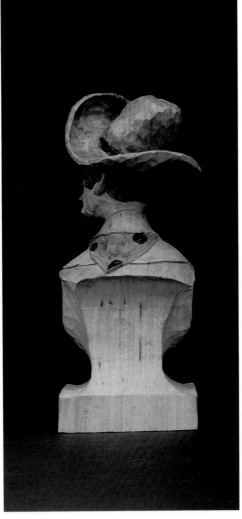

Sippin' Sid

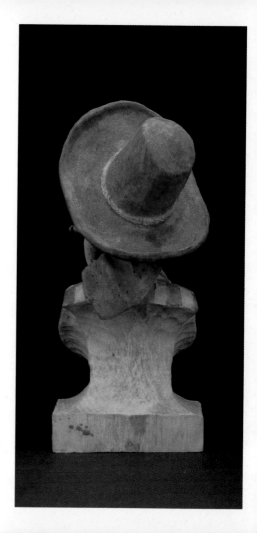

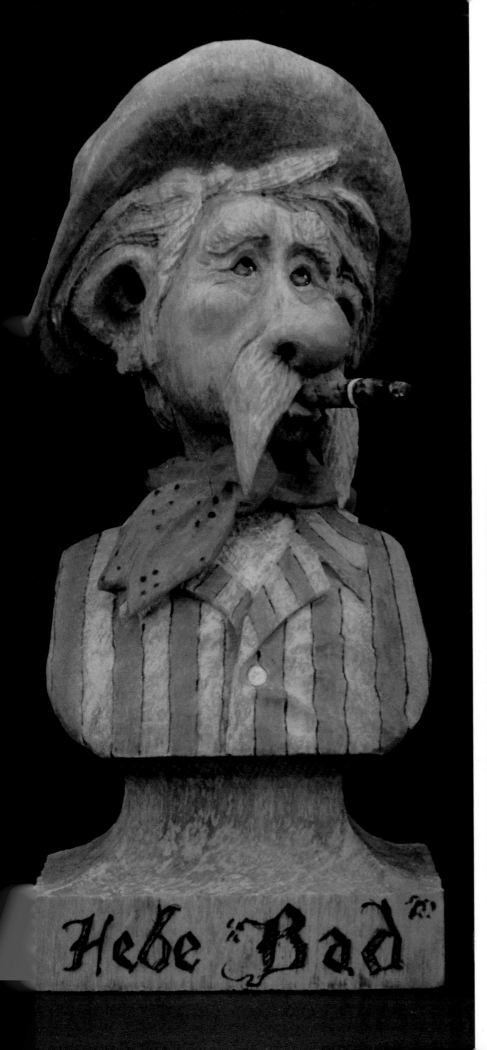

56

The Soiled Dove

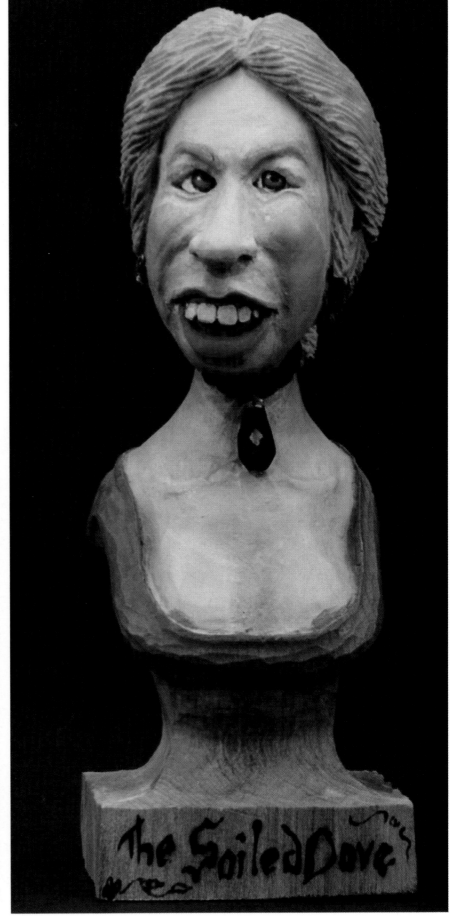

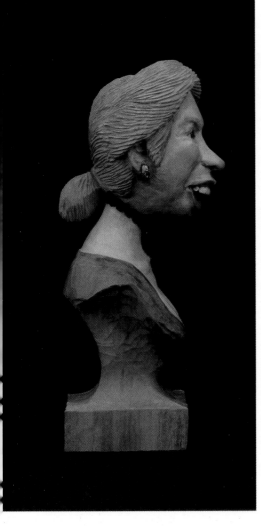

Billy Blue

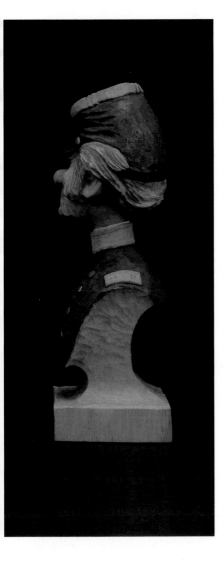

The Gunner

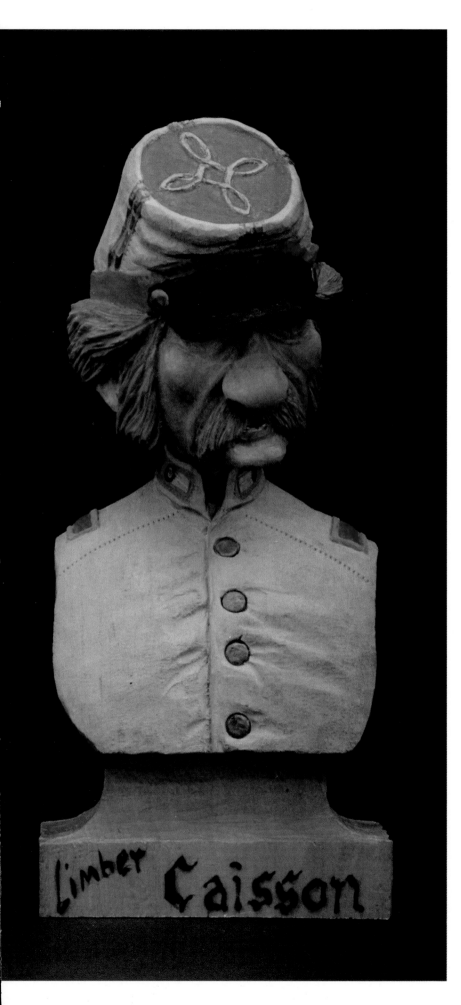

Limber Caisson

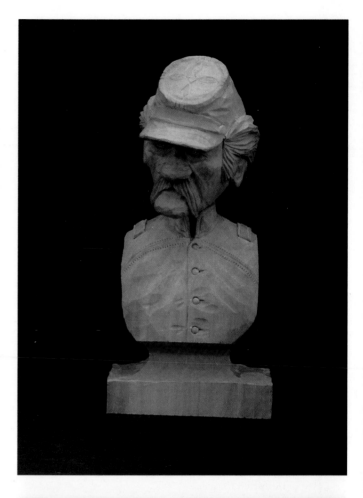
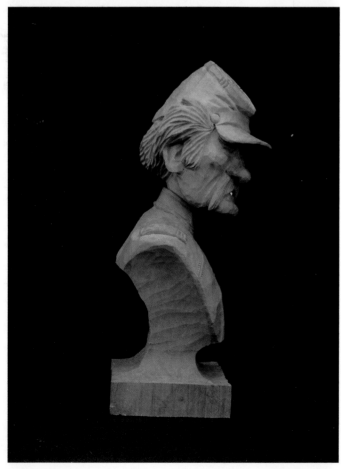